Nov. 9, 2007

Peiling and the
Chicken-Fried Christmas

Peiling and the Chicken-Fried Christmas

PAULINE CHEN

BLOOMSBURY
CHILDREN'S
BOOKS

Published by Bloomsbury U.S.A. Children's Books
175 Fifth Avenue, New York, NY 10010
Distributed to the trade by Holtzbrinck Publishers

Library of Congress Cataloging-in-Publication Data
Chen, Pauline.
Peiling and the chicken-fried Christmas / by Pauline Chen. — 1st U.S. ed.
        p.   cm.
Summary: Fifth-grader Peiling Wang wants to celebrate "a real American Christmas,"
much to the displeasure of her traditional, Taiwanese-born father.
ISBN-13: 978-1-59990-122-0 • ISBN-10: 1-59990-122-6
1. Taiwanese Americans—Juvenile fiction. [1. Taiwanese Americans—Fiction.
2. Christmas—Fiction.]   I. Title.
PZ7.C41814Pe 2007   [Fic]—dc22   2006102095

First U.S. Edition 2007
Typeset by Westchester Book Composition
Printed in the U.S.A. by Quebecor World Fairfield
2 4 6 8 10 9 7 5 3 1

All papers used by Bloomsbury U.S.A. are natural, recyclable products
made from wood grown in well-managed forests. The manufacturing processes
conform to the environmental regulations of the country of origin.

In memory of
Yan-Yan Hwang and Yu-Chen Gau

Peiling and the
Chicken-Fried Christmas

1

Dear Miss Rosenweig:
Please excuse Peiling from class the first day of school after Christmas vacation. Listening to all the other kids brag about their Christmas gifts makes her stomach turn . . .

Peiling Wang leaned back in her chair and read over what she had written. She pictured herself going downstairs and asking Mama to sign it. *"You what? Wang Peiling, are you crazy?"* Peiling crumpled up the paper and threw it in the wastebasket. Then she looked out the window at the leafless trees against the gray sky.

It was here again, her least favorite time of the year. December, which seemed to come earlier and earlier every year, even before the Wangs had finished eating all their leftover duck from Thanksgiving. December, when everywhere and everything chorused *Christmas*: the cutout reindeer on the neighbors' lawn, the piped-in carols at the dentist's office, the fake-bearded Santa endlessly ringing a bell in front of the post office. It was December, and everyone was getting ready for Christmas. Everyone, that is, but the Wangs.

"Come down for breakfast, Peiling!" Mama yelled from the bottom of the stairs. "Your soy milk's getting cold."

Peiling got reluctantly to her feet, shoved her schoolbooks in her backpack, and ran downstairs.

In the kitchen, Baba was listening gloomily to the weather report as he ate his *youtiao,* a long stick of salty fried dough. He dunked one end into his bowl of soy milk then bit off the moistened part, his jaw moving steadily as his eyes stared into empty space.

"Don't you have Drama Club this morning?" Mama asked.

Peiling nodded, sliding into her place, where a big bowl of soy milk was already steaming gently.

Mama glanced at the clock. "Then you'd better hurry or we'll be late." She plunked half a bagel spread with cream cheese in front of Peiling.

Peiling covertly watched Baba as he popped the last bites of *youtiao* into his mouth. She tried to imagine him as a boy getting excited about the holidays, say, Chinese

New Year or the Dragon Boat Festival. "Did you ever celebrate Christmas when you were little, Baba?" she asked, a little shyly.

Baba pulled a handkerchief from the pocket of his baggy trousers and wiped his greasy fingers on it. Baba considered it an appalling waste the way people in America would wipe their mouth or hands on a paper napkin, and then just throw it away. Even when he killed an ant or a spider that had wandered into the house, he would tear off the teeniest possible scrap from the corner of a paper towel to squish it.

"In Taiwan?" he said, tucking the handkerchief back into his pocket. "In Taiwan, the American soldiers at the military base gave out chocolate and tins of butter on Christmas. We had never eaten such things before. They gave me a terrible case of the runs."

His voice sharpened. "That's salt, not sugar."

"What?" she said, confused.

"You just put salt into your soy milk instead of sugar."

She looked around the kitchen table. Baba was right. The small china canister in which Mama put salt was right next to the sugar bowl. She had just stuck her spoon into the wrong one.

Mama came bustling over. "Don't worry. I'll throw it out and give you a new bowl."

Baba stopped Mama on the way to the sink. "No, that's all right. I'll drink it." He took Peiling's bowl. He pushed his own bowl, still nearly full, toward Peiling. With a deep sigh, he put her bowl to his lips. He grimaced and shut his eyes, but kept on drinking.

Peiling looked longingly at the sugar bowl, but felt too guilty to add sugar to the bowl he had given her. She began to spoon it into her mouth plain.

The weather report ended. A slow, old-time version of "The Christmas Song" came on next. It was Peiling's favorite Christmas carol. As the singer's deep, melting voice filled the kitchen, her eyes fluttered shut and she felt her body sink into the hard kitchen chair.

Chestnuts roasting on an open fire
Jack Frost nipping at your nose . . .

Baba reached over and clicked off the radio. "It's supposed to snow today. Better drive carefully," he told Mama. He got up and put his empty bowl in the sink. He kissed Mama absently, and patted Peiling on the head. Then he disappeared into the garage, buttoning up his overcoat.

Seconds later, there was a frantic screech of tires in the driveway. The side door banged open, and Uncle Samson bounded in without knocking. "Morning, everyone!" He plopped a stack of Chinese DVDs he had borrowed over the weekend on the counter. "Just dropping these by on the way to work."

Baba's angry face popped back through the door to the garage. "Do you know that you're blocking the garage door?" he growled at Uncle Samson in Taiwanese. "How am I supposed to get to work?"

"Oh, sorry," Uncle Samson responded in English. He shot out the side door and Peiling heard the powerful engine of his Mitsubishi sports car starting up.

"Turbo? Who needs turbo?" Baba grumbled to himself. "What is this, the Indy 500?" He stomped back into the garage. A moment later they heard Baba's car start, its muffler clanking noisily against the curb as Baba pulled out of the driveway.

Uncle Samson came back into the kitchen.

"Have you had breakfast?" Mama asked him.

"I had a cup of coffee."

"Coffee's not breakfast." Mama was already putting another bagel in the toaster. "How can you sit in front of a computer all morning on an empty stomach?" Uncle Samson was Mama's youngest brother. Even though he was in his mid-twenties, all the other aunties and uncles bossed him around and treated him like he was a child.

Taking off his suede jacket, Uncle Samson straddled the kitchen chair beside Peiling. "Wanna go skating sometime after school?" he said.

"Sure," Peiling said, her face lighting up. She loved to do things with Uncle Samson.

"How about Wednesday?"

"Okay," said Peiling.

Mama poured Uncle Samson a glass of soy milk. She sat down on the other side of him. "Good," she approved. "You can come to dinner afterwards." She pointed at the stack of DVDs. "Did you watch them all?" she asked casually.

Uncle Samson nodded, sipping his soy milk.

"So you must not have had much to do this weekend," Mama said. "No hot dates?"

Peiling squirmed. She hated when Mama used slang words like "hot date," enunciating them with overdone precision as if she were speaking a foreign language.

Uncle Samson ignored Mama. He got the bagel out of the toaster himself and began to spread it with cream cheese.

"You know, you should really get over Cindy," Mama went on. Cindy was the name of Uncle Samson's ex-girlfriend. "How long has it been since you broke up? Ten months, a year?"

Uncle Samson was silent.

"Besides, she just wasn't right for you," Mama continued. "She was *sanba* . . . what's the word? Bubble-brain?"

Uncle Samson didn't look at Mama. "Airhead," he said shortly.

"Exactly. Well, anyway—"

"Look, Shuli, I don't want to talk about it." Looking harassed, Uncle Samson shrugged his jacket back on. He gulped down the rest of the soy milk and wrapped the bagel in a paper napkin so he could eat it in the car.

"But there's lots of other nice girls around. You should—"

Peiling got to her feet, clearing her throat noisily. "Mama, if we don't leave now, I'm going to be late," she said.

Mama looked at the clock and jumped. "You're right." She threw on her coat and grabbed her car keys. As Peiling followed Mama through the door to the garage, she looked back.

Uncle Samson was staring down into the bottom of his empty mug. But when he caught Peiling looking at him, he quickly put on a goofy grin. "Whew!" he mouthed at her, pretending to wipe sweat from his brow. "Thanks, Peiling!"

2

"Let's start with Act One. Places, everyone!" Mrs. Baldino trilled, hobbling to the center of the stage, trailing clouds of a heavy scent. To Peiling, it smelled like a flowery version of Kool-Aid, but Mrs. Baldino always called it "toilet water." The drama teacher flipped open her curled and dog-eared script of *The Prince and the Pauper*. She peered at it through tortoiseshell glasses.

"Madeline, you go stage left." Madeline Downs, the kindergartner who was playing the pauper's little sister, stopped sucking her thumb and toddled over to her place.

"Matthew, you're stage right."

Matt Denn, who played the pauper's father, didn't move. Peiling saw that he was staring dreamily at a spider spinning a web in a corner of the pauper's hovel.

Mrs. Baldino sighed. She steered him by the shoulders to the right side of the stage.

"Now, Matthew," she said firmly, stooping down so that her face was at his level. "Today I want you to really *emote.*" She scrunched up her face into a grimace, and clenched one hand into a tight fist. "I want you to *find* Mr. Canty's anger, deep inside of you . . ."

"But Mrs. Baldino," Laura Hamilton interrupted, squeezing herself past where Peiling was painting scenery through a gap in the walls of the pauper's hovel. "Simon's not here!" Her words, uttered in a piercing voice, seemed to echo through the entire auditorium. Laura was playing the prince. Even though she didn't appear until the second act, she was already wearing her gold-sequined crown and red velvet robe.

"Not here? Again?" said Mrs. Baldino blankly. She gazed around the stage. Her gnarled hand fell limply to her side, still gripping the script. Simon Pence was playing the pauper. "Are you sure?"

Laura nodded. She seemed almost pleased with herself, as if being the bearer of bad news made her more important. She continued relentlessly, "And this is the third time he's missed rehearsal . . ."

"And the performance is the last week in January!" Mrs. Baldino quavered. She tottered over to a chair at the edge of the stage and clutched it for support. "My last play before I retire," she murmured. "I did so want it to be my masterpiece . . ." Her knees buckled beneath her and she collapsed into the chair.

Matthew and Madeline looked at each other nervously over her inert form. Peiling looked at Laura accusingly.

Mrs. Baldino suddenly lifted her head a few inches. "Peiling?" she whispered.

"Yes?" Peiling, startled, almost dropped her paint-brush.

"Could I trouble you to read the pauper's part today?" Mrs. Baldino spoke faintly, as if she hardly had the breath to form the words.

Peiling wiped her paint-covered hands on a rag, pleased. This year, she had finally gotten up the nerve to sign up for tryouts. She had wanted to play Grandam Canty, the pauper's grandmother. But then it turned out that Mama had scheduled a dentist's appointment for her the afternoon of tryouts, and Peiling hadn't been able to go. "Sure," she said, putting the paintbrush down on a wad of newspaper.

"Superb!" Mrs. Baldino bounced up from the chair, her energy restored. She dragged the pauper's tattered costume on over Peiling's jeans and sweater, and placed her hands on either side of Peiling's head. "Close your eyes," she ordered.

"Now, you are the pauper," Mrs. Baldino intoned, gently massaging Peiling's temples. "Your father is a thief and drunkard. You've had nothing to eat all day but dry bread and water. You haven't had a bath in months, and you probably—no, almost certainly— have lice . . ." Peiling's hand reached up automatically to scratch her head. Mrs. Baldino handed Peiling her own script and thrust her center stage. "Now knock 'em dead."

Peiling stared down at the first page. Every inch of available space was scribbled with Mrs. Baldino's notes and stage directions: *Grit teeth and clench fists!* and *With feeling!* After a panicked moment, she found the pauper's first line. "Oh, Father," she began haltingly. "I brought home only a farthing, although I begged all day up and down Mincing Lane . . ."

"A farthing! A paltry farthing!" Matthew growled. He gritted his teeth, clenched his fists and advanced on Peiling menacingly. "By my troth, methinks I'll tan thy good-for-nothing hide!"

It was just the sort of old-fashioned play Mrs. Baldino loved, crowded with men in doublets and women in bodices, and chock-full of "thee's" and "thou's" and "prithee, sirrahs." All the other kids in Drama Club made fun of the way the characters talked. For instance, whenever Simon Pence saw Laura, he called her "comely damsel," and bowed and pretended to take off his hat. Laura would always be furious.

But in her heart of hearts, Peiling secretly liked the play because of its wacky, far-fetched plot. It was about two boys, born on the very same day, who by a strange co-incidence happened to look exactly alike. One, Tom Canty, was a neglected beggar in the meanest slum; while the other, Prince Edward, was the pampered heir to the throne of England. When the two meet by chance and try on each other's clothes for fun, Tom is mistaken for the Prince, while Edward, in tatters, is turned out of the palace to make his own way.

At first Peiling stumbled painfully over the unfamiliar words. But then as she spoke them, the words seemed to take on a life of their own, and she heard her own voice grow louder and clearer.

"Mother dear, when I first lay down, I couldn't sleep, because I was sorely hungry, and aching from my father's beatings," she read. "But then I fell into a deep, sweet slumber, and had the most wondrous of dreams. I dreamt of a castle, with servants, and pleasure gardens all laid out . . ."

As she read the words, she could feel all at once the suffering, the meanness, of the pauper's life. She gazed past the painted backdrops and cardboard props to picture the pile of dirty straw on which he slept, the crusts of dry bread he gnawed, the crowded, narrow, sunless streets where he begged. She imagined how cold he would get in the winter in his rags and tatters; how he would reach his hands, stiff and frozen, toward the fire, only to be cuffed away roughly by his father. She understood why he would take refuge in dreams of luxury. The pauper's feelings became so vivid to her that when she came to the last line of the act, "Oh, that I should one day, with my very own eyes, see a real prince," she could hear her own voice break with longing.

"Lovely, lovely!" Mrs. Baldino came onstage, applauding so enthusiastically that her earrings jangled. "That was quite, quite lovely. I didn't know you could read with so much feeling, Peiling." She patted Peiling's shoulder approvingly. "I wonder if we shouldn't make you Simon's understudy."

Before Peiling could open her mouth to say yes, Laura Hamilton came swishing onstage in her velvet robes again. "But Mrs. Baldino," she opened her script and jabbed at a line. "It says right here on page five that Tom is supposed to have fair hair. Besides, there weren't any Chinese people in England back then, were there?" She wrinkled her brow with the effort of recollection. "I mean, it's the sixteenth century . . ."

"Now, Laura, there's no need to be so literal—"

"People didn't have braces in the sixteenth century, either," Peiling muttered, looking pointedly at the brackets and wires on Laura's teeth.

Laura ignored Peiling and continued talking to Mrs. Baldino. "But the real problem is, Peiling and I don't look anything alike. The prince and the pauper are supposed to look exactly alike, you know." She spoke, as always, with slow, exaggerated motions of her mouth, as if everyone else were hard of hearing. "That's how come they can be mistaken for each other."

She turned to Peiling, gesturing at her own long blonde hair with one hand, and pointing to Peiling's straight black bob with the other. "No offense, Peiling, but you and I look totally different."

"What's there to feel offended about?" Peiling said.

"What do you mean?"

"Why should I feel offended that we don't look alike?" Peiling said.

Laura looked at her uncomprehendingly.

"Why should you assume that I want to look like you, and not that you want to look like me . . ." Peiling floundered, trailing off lamely. She knew that she had a point. She just wasn't sure she could express it with the whole Drama Club goggling curiously at her.

"Girls, girls," Mrs. Baldino interceded. "I'm sure that with costumes and makeup we can take care of everything. And Simon will probably be back in a day or two . . ."

Ignoring the part about Simon, Laura looked at Peiling with her head tilted to one side. "Yeah," she muttered, nodding critically. "I guess a blonde wig would help. But her eyes . . ."

Peiling felt her face getting red. She wanted to make some angry retort, but she couldn't think of a single word to say. "What about my eyes?" she choked.

The morning bell rang. The rehearsal was over. It was time to go to their classrooms. Mrs. Baldino, clearly relieved, was flapping her script, trying to get everyone's attention over the flurry of kids collecting their bookbags and coats. "Don't forget—rehearsal next Monday!"

"Hey, Peiling," Laura said. Peiling ignored her. Even though they were both going to Miss Rosenweig's classroom, Peiling headed quickly out of the auditorium without waiting for Laura.

Peiling could name the very hour and minute she had begun to hate Laura. It had been the first week of fifth grade. They were starting off the year with a unit on exotic plants, and Miss Rosenweig had asked the kids to bring in any unusual plants they had at home. Peiling had brought in Mama's orchid with its spike of pale mauve flowers. Even though orchids were easy to grow in Taiwan, it was very hard to keep them alive in the colder, drier climate of Ohio.

Peiling had just carried the orchid to the front of the room and begun to explain how Mama put it in front of a south-facing window, and misted it with a spray bottle morning and evening, when Laura bustled to the front of the room with her plant.

"This is a Venus flytrap. It's a carnivorous plant," Laura had announced. It was in a glass terrarium. Laura had brought a live fly in a glass jar. Before Miss Rosenweig could stop her, she shook the fly into the terrarium, and the whole class gathered around excitedly to see whether the flytrap would catch it. Peiling's orchid was forgotten.

That incident pretty much summed up Laura Hamilton in a nutshell. She was a know-it-all and a show-off. When Miss Rosenweig asked for a volunteer for a task or an errand, Laura was so desperate to hog all the credit that she nearly bodychecked any other kid who tried to get ahead of her. She loved to ridicule other people. Whenever someone mispronounced a word in

Spanish class, Laura smirked and rolled her eyes at the Spanish teacher, as if the two of them shared some special secret.

Laura had strong points, too, Peiling tried to remind herself. She was a good actress, and had an excellent singing voice. She had starred in almost every school play, from *Little Red Riding Hood* in first grade, to *Annie* last year. She was also one of the best students in the whole grade. But the truth was, these things didn't make Peiling like Laura more. In fact, they only made it even easier to hate her.

3

In Miss Rosenweig's classroom, Peiling slid into her seat beside her best friend, Grace.

"Hi, Peiling," Grace muttered, barely looking up. As usual, she was filling the blank pages at the back of her notebook with elaborate doodles.

"What are you drawing?" Peiling asked, taking her own notebook out of her backpack.

"It's a space station on the surface of one of the moons of Saturn," Grace replied, carefully using her mechanical pencil to draw flames shooting out of a rocket thruster. Everyone said that Grace was exceptionally talented. The art teacher was always trying to get her to do "still lifes" of jugs of wine and bunches of grapes. But every free moment she got, Grace covered her notebooks with geometric, futuristic-looking structures and intergalactic battles.

"Good morning, everyone!" Miss Rosenweig burst into the classroom. She took off her fluorescent lime-green bike helmet and shook out her long waves of curly brown hair. Her brown velvet coat was appliquéd with huge red roses. Even in the middle of winter she wore Birkenstock sandals over chunky, hand-knit, striped socks. Peiling could never figure out whether other people thought Miss Rosenweig looked crazy or stylish. To her, Miss Rosenweig always looked beautiful.

Miss Rosenweig tore off the November page from the large calendar next to the blackboard, revealing the month of December. Peiling turned her eyes away to avoid seeing the bright-red "25."

"In just a few weeks," Miss Rosenweig said, "it'll be the Winter Solstice. Does anyone know what that is?"

The class was silent.

"The Winter Solstice?" Grace glanced up casually from her picture. It was one of Grace's peculiarities that she never seemed to realize that teachers might not like her drawing in class. "The Winter Solstice is the day of the year when the night is longest, and the hours of daylight are the shortest. It's usually the first day of winter, around December twenty-first or so."

"Excellent!" Miss Rosenweig nodded enthusiastically. "I love your pictures, Grace," she added pleasantly. "But would you mind saving them for after class?" Miss Rosenweig never humiliated students when she corrected them; she was a big believer in "mutual respect." Grace sheepishly put her picture away.

"And all over the world," Miss Rosenweig continued, "people celebrate different holidays in honor of the

Winter Solstice. And I don't just mean Christmas and Hanukkah. Does anybody here celebrate one?"

Miss Rosenweig's sparkling brown eyes looked expectantly around the room. Was it just her imagination, or did they seem to rest on Peiling? Peiling forced her hand up a few inches.

"Yes, Peiling?"

"We celebrate Chinese New Year," she offered reluctantly. "It's not the same time as the American New Year. It's usually in late January or February."

Laura, who sat two rows ahead, slewed around in her seat to stare at Peiling. "You mean you don't celebrate Christmas?"

Peiling sank lower in her seat and shook her head. Laura was looking at her like she was one of the creatures inhabiting Grace's space station.

"Neither does half the world, Laura," Miss Rosenweig reminded her. She smiled at Peiling encouragingly. "Why don't you tell the class what you do for Chinese New Year?"

The last thing Peiling wanted to do was reveal the peculiar things her family did to the rest of the class. "The week before New Year's you have to clean up the whole house," she mumbled, looking down. "Then on New Year's Day we put on new clothes and visit relatives. Then we go to a Chinese restaurant and watch the lion dancers, and everyone sets off firecrackers to scare the evil spirits away in the new year."

"Firecrackers—awesome!" Steven Plaxe yelled from across the aisle.

"Do you get any presents?" Sandra Park wanted to know.

"I don't get presents, but my parents and aunts and uncles give me money in red envelopes."

"How much?" Laura said, at the same moment Steven said, "Cash. Now that's cool."

"Do you eat anything special?" asked Miss Rosenweig.

"We eat a sticky, gooey rice cake, called *nian gao*, because the word for 'sticky' sounds the same as the word for 'year.'" Out of the corner of her eye Peiling thought she saw Laura giggling with Steven when she said the word *nian gao*, but she resolutely tried to ignore them.

"That sounds delicious," said Miss Rosenweig, beaming. "I hope I get to try some. In fact, maybe you can bring some in for the class to sample in January. Thank you, Peiling, for sharing your holiday traditions with the class. Anyone else?"

No one said anything.

"Then let's take a look at some other holiday traditions from some other places from around the globe. Someone, please pull down the screen." Peiling rose to do it. Laura quickly cut ahead of her to yank it down, so Peiling turned out the lights instead. Miss Rosenweig turned on the slide projector.

In the darkened room, images of Miss Rosenweig lighting a menorah, spinning a dreidel, and frying potato latkes flashed on-screen. Peiling gazed, fascinated. She had always assumed that Miss Rosenweig, like everyone else she knew, celebrated Christmas.

"My family's Jewish, and we celebrate Hanukkah," Miss Rosenweig explained. "These are pictures of me celebrating Hanukkah on a kibbutz, or communal farm, in Israel. I lived there for a year after college."

Suddenly there was a pop, and the screen went blank.

"Oh, no. The bulb must have blown!" Miss Rosenweig exclaimed. "Could someone go next door to Mr. Guy's and see if we can borrow his projector?" This time, Sandra, who had a crush on Mr. Guy, managed to beat Laura to the door.

A moment later, Mr. Guy, the other fifth-grade teacher, appeared with a slide projector. He was about Miss Rosenweig's age, and wore octagonal steel-rimmed glasses and narrow-legged black jeans.

"I can't believe you're still using this thing, Deanna," he said, placing his projector on the table and plugging it in. "Mine's been sitting in the closet gathering dust the whole year."

He transferred the carousel of slides from the broken projector to the new one. "It's a lot easier to just digitize your photos, you know. I'd be happy to show you how sometime."

He turned the projector on. A picture of Miss Rosenweig wearing a colorful tunic and pants on a crowded street flashed on-screen. Holding her hand was a dark-haired, dark-eyed young man in a turban.

"Who's that?" said Mr. Guy sharply.

"Oops, how did that get in here?" Miss Rosenweig muttered, blushing and quickly clicking to the next slide. This one showed a glittering palace with domes and turrets thronged by people. "Shouldn't you be getting back to your class?" she said. Mr. Guy left with a grumpy expression on his face.

"This is a picture of Sikh worshippers going to the Golden Temple in the Punjab on Diwali, the Festival of Lights," Miss Rosenweig said. Peiling noticed that her face was still a little red. "Diwali is an especially important holiday in India, because it's celebrated by Hindus, Sikhs, and Jains. On Diwali, *diyas*, or oil lights, are lit to symbolize the triumph of light over darkness, or evil."

Miss Rosenweig clicked the switch to show a new photo of her sitting on a cushion next to a low table covered by plates of unfamiliar-looking foods. "This is me celebrating Ramadan, a Muslim festival, with Khadija, my roommate from grad school. We've just fasted and read passages from the Koran all day, and now it's sundown, and we're about to have *harira*, a kind of chickpea soup. I traveled all over the world the year after I finished my master's degree," she explained, as she clicked through a few more pictures. "I stayed with Khadija's family in Cairo, Egypt, for a month. I also spent some time in India," she added. She shut off the projector and turned on the lights. "Any questions?"

Laura Hamilton asked the question on everyone's mind. "Was that guy in the picture your boyfriend?"

Peiling cringed. Laura was so tactless. Yet Peiling listened breathlessly for Miss Rosenweig's reply.

"He used to be," Miss Rosenweig answered, blushing some more. "But things didn't work out. His parents . . ." she trailed off. She shook her head, as if brushing off a bad memory.

"But the real reason I brought in these pictures was to talk about our Winter Project." Every year, all the classes in school, from the kindergartners to the sixth graders, had to do a Winter Project. They would be put on display at the Winter Assembly, when the school play—this year, *The Prince and the Pauper*—would also be performed. Miss Rosenweig went back to the calendar and flipped a page. "Let's see. The Winter Assembly is on the evening of January twenty-fifth. That's just seven weeks from now."

"Here's my idea," Miss Rosenweig said. Her eyes, momentarily dimmed by Laura's question, had grown big and sparkling again. "We'll do a collage called 'How the World Celebrates,' with pictures and symbols of holidays from all around the world!"

Peiling sensed all the kids in the class fidgeting uneasily. Fortunately, Laura again raised her hand and asked the question on everybody's mind. "How about something to do with Christmas?" she said. "That's what everyone else does for their Winter Project."

"But that's why it's so boring," Miss Rosenweig retorted. "And it doesn't take into consideration our rich multicultural tapestry. Besides," she added, "does anyone really want to hear 'We Three Kings' in late January?"

Peiling had to admit that Miss Rosenweig had a point, even though she had looked forward to doing a Christmas project too. Laura, however, didn't give up so easily. "But Miss Rosenweig, I heard Mrs. Daniels's class is doing a gingerbread crèche. Isn't that the way to go? You know, kind of a new twist on something traditional . . ."

Miss Rosenweig ignored Laura. "Now, this is what I was thinking. For the background, I want images of people and places from all around the world." She raised her hands with outspread fingers and shut her eyes with a dreamy smile as she pictured it. "I want everyone to cut out pictures from magazines and newspapers, and then we'll paste them on a big piece of plywood.

"And in the foreground," here she opened her eyes and paused for dramatic effect. "You know how, according to the Chinese calendar, it'll be the Year of the Chicken? So how about a giant chicken, right in the middle?"

Peiling and Grace looked at one another, stunned. Then the two of them looked at the rest of the class. Every face was overspread with the same expression of horror and dismay.

Miss Rosenweig bubbled on, oblivious to the agony she was inspiring. "So how about we dye some macaroni, make a mosaic . . ."

4

"Macaroni?" Peiling muttered to Grace, as they walked to the lunchroom. "We're going to present a project made out of macaroni to the entire school?"

"I knew she was low-tech," agreed Grace. "But macaroni?" Grace shook her head.

"I mean, does she even know how to use a computer?" Sandra demanded indignantly, catching up to them.

"There's that one on her desk," said Peiling.

"But I've never actually seen her touch it," Grace said.

"Does she even know how to drive a car?" Sandra asked. "Maybe that's why she rides her bike to school, even in the middle of winter."

"I think that's because she's worried about greenhouse emissions," Peiling said.

"But our Winter Project sounds awful. Mr. Guy is going to think we're such losers . . ."

Peiling and Grace rolled their eyes at each other as Sandra went to stand in the lunch line. It usually took only a few minutes for Sandra to return to her favorite topic of conversation: Mr. Guy. The two of them went to their usual round table in the corner.

As Peiling pulled out a Tupperware of duck fried rice, Grace took out the same lunch she brought every day: an American cheese sandwich on white bread, a hard-boiled egg, and a banana. Together, the foods made a symphony of yellow and white. Peiling used to think that it was strange that someone so creative had such a boring diet. But then she had come to realize that Grace had such a wild and fevered imagination, that she actually craved some routine in life.

"But I'm afraid Sandra's right," Peiling said, unscrewing her thermos of egg-drop soup. "I bet it's going to be a total disaster."

"Ah, well," said Grace philosophically. "True creativity is always a matter of trial and error . . . Look what I found at a garage sale this weekend," Grace, who collected comic books, pulled out her latest acquisition. "It's the first Captain America, way back from the forties." She pointed to the picture of Captain America in skintight spandex on the cover. "Look at the way he's drawn," Grace said enthusiastically. "You can make out every one of his muscles: pecs, glutes, quads. He could be a model in an anatomy text book."

As Peiling bent to look, a piercing voice beside her ear said, "Can you believe Miss Rosenweig?"

Peiling jumped. It was Laura Hamilton. She sat down at their table. Peiling was surprised; she had certainly never done so before. "I mean, *hello?*" Laura continued, "People actually *like* Christmas. No one's interested in—whatever you call it—Diwali."

Glancing at the neatly wrapped tuna fish sandwich and box of cranberry juice that Laura pulled out of her lunch bag, Peiling suddenly felt self-conscious about her own lunch. For a moment, she was tempted to put her food away before Laura noticed it and started making comments. She forced herself to keep eating.

"We'll be the laughingstock of the whole entire school," Laura went on. "Hey, Britney! Hey, Emma!" Laura yelled across the lunchroom, catching sight of her two best friends. "Come and sit with us!"

Britney Lewis and Emma Fox, who were in Mr. Guy's class, made their way over.

As they put their trays on the table and sat down, Laura said disgustedly, "Have you heard about our Winter Project?"

The two girls shook their heads.

"A collage called 'How the World Celebrates,' with a giant chicken in the middle!" Laura said bitterly.

In fulfillment of Laura's dire prediction that they would be the school laughingstock, Britney and Emma started to giggle.

"Miss Rosenweig is so weird," Britney said. "Remember last spring? She made her class opt out of the fifth-grade soccer tournament and do a yoga demonstration instead."

Peiling did remember. Miss Rosenweig's class had

done a series of "sun salutations" and "cobra poses" to a recording of twanging sitar music. Mr. Guy's class had won the tournament by forfeit, even though they weren't very good.

"And what about that Thanksgiving potluck two weeks ago?" Emma chimed in. "What'd your class make? Some kind of weird, healthy thing . . ."

"Vegan soy milk pumpkin spelt muffins," Laura said grimly.

Peiling's stomach hurt a little, just thinking about those muffins. The recipe had sounded good, but when the muffins came out of the oven, they had turned out to be as dense and heavy as rocks.

Peiling noticed Britney and Emma glancing at each other with smug expressions. "Have you heard about *our* Winter Project?" Britney said.

"What are you guys doing?" Laura demanded.

"We're doing a video installation," Britney said.

"What's that?" Peiling asked.

"Mr. Guy is going to bring in a digital camcorder, and we're going to make a video," Britney began.

"It'll be called 'Christmas Is . . . ' " Emma continued. "And everyone in the class will be on camera talking about how they feel about Christmas!"

"Isn't Simon Pence in your class?" Grace said. "That'll be really gripping. Christmas is . . ." Grace imitated Simon's droning monotone, "da bomb."

Emma and Britney looked annoyed.

Bored with the conversation, Grace drew Peiling's attention back to her comic book. "Look at the perspective in this picture. It's low, so it makes the buildings look even taller . . ."

"Hey, Peiling," Laura interrupted suddenly.

Peiling looked up guardedly, her mouth full of duck fried rice.

"We're baking Christmas cookies at my house this week," Laura said. "Since you don't celebrate Christmas yourself, I was wondering if you wanted to come."

Peiling stared at Laura, amazed. She had hated admitting in front of Laura, of all people, that she didn't celebrate Christmas, because she was certain that Laura would make fun of her. She searched Laura's expression intently, but as far as she could see, there was no mockery on Laura's pale, freckled face with its rabbit teeth. If anything, she looked a little nervous. Hastily swallowing her mouthful of rice, Peiling nodded.

"Great." Laura smiled, flashing her braces. "How about you, Grace?"

Grace nodded. "Sure."

"How's Friday afternoon?" Laura said. "You can come home with me on my bus after school."

After Laura had finished her lunch and gone off between Britney and Emma, Grace commented, "I'm glad you're coming to Laura's house. You've always had kind of a thing about her."

"I do not have a thing about her," Peiling said.

"Yes, you do. But she's really not that bad." Grace lived a few doors down from Laura, and had known her since they were little kids. "Actually, my mom says she's kind of insecure. That's why she always acts a little self-centered."

"A *little* self-centered?" Peiling said incredulously. "You know what she's like? A black hole. Except instead of sucking up matter, she sucks up attention."

Grace laughed. "Yeah, but you just have to know how to take her."

"Yeah, in really small doses," Peiling said.

5

The sun was slipping down behind the trees at the western end of the rink.

"Last time around. I'll race you," Uncle Samson called. He darted off, skating backwards, while Peiling skated forwards. He zigzagged on his hockey skates, looking over his shoulder to make sure he didn't bump into anyone. The rink was almost empty now anyway.

Usually if Peiling tried her best, she could beat him. But today, somehow her skates felt heavy and clumsy on her feet. As they were rounding the last curve, she lunged forward to pass him, but he blocked her and got to the goalpost first.

"Slowpoke," he panted. He slowed down so that she could catch up to him. "Do you want a hot chocolate?"

Peiling hesitated. She knew Mama would say that it would spoil her appetite, but she wasn't quite ready to go home yet. "All right." She skated after Uncle Samson toward the snack bar at the other end of the rink.

"Two hot chocolates," Uncle Samson said to the girl

at the snack bar, who was dressed as one of Santa's elves. She handed them two steaming cups.

"What's biting you, Peiling?" Uncle Samson said, as they sat down on a bench beneath the trees to drink them. He was the only one of the aunts and uncles who could use slang in a halfway convincing way. Peiling thought it was because he had been younger, still a teenager, when he came over from Taiwan to the States. "You've hardly said a word all afternoon."

Peiling gazed at the Christmas lights, just coming on in the gathering darkness around the edge of the rink. They cast pools of color, red and green and gold, blending together on the surface of the ice. She didn't drink her hot chocolate, just sat there looking at the lights. She wanted to talk to him about what Laura had said about her hair and eyes at rehearsal, about Miss Rosenweig making her tell the class about Chinese New Year. Only she didn't know how to put into words what had happened, and how it made her feel. So instead she only said, without looking at him, "I wish we celebrated Christmas."

Uncle Samson stuck out his tongue to fish a mini-marshmallow from his hot chocolate. He chewed it thoughtfully. "Well, why don't you ask your parents if you can celebrate it?" he suggested.

"Well, I hinted about it last year—," she began.

"Hinted!" Uncle Samson said. "There's a darn sight too much hinting going on in this family, if you ask me. Why don't you come straight out and ask them?"

She hesitated, and then said hopelessly, "Why bother? You know they'll say no."

"Why do you think so?"

"They always say no when I ask them if I can do stuff that everyone else is doing."

"Give me an example."

"Like getting my ears pierced, like seeing PG-13 movies, like wearing makeup, like getting cable," Peiling counted on her fingers.

Uncle Samson laughed. "Well, I can understand their saying no to all those things. Except getting your ears pierced." Uncle Samson had a pierced ear in which he wore a little gold stud. "But that doesn't mean that you shouldn't ask them about Christmas if that's what you really want," he continued.

Peiling was silent. Of course she wanted to celebrate Christmas. She wanted it more than almost anything in the world. At the same time, something told her that asking Mama and Baba about Christmas was somehow different from asking them about pierced ears or cable TV. There was a Chinese saying that Mama liked to use, *yi dao, liang duan*, or "One knife cut, then two broken pieces." It meant an absolute decision, one from which there was no turning back. That was what asking them about Christmas would be like.

Uncle Samson seemed to guess how she felt without her explaining. "Look, Peiling," he said gently. "I know you're just a kid. But you're old enough to have a conversation with your parents, to let them know who you are."

"Who I am?" she echoed dubiously.

"Who you are, what you want. And maybe that's different from who they are and what they want for you."

It all sounded so reasonable when he said it. "But don't you think they'll say no to Christmas?" Peiling pursued, wanting him to contradict her.

"I don't really know what they'll say. Well, your dad can be a little stubborn. But your mom . . ." He trailed off, meditatively sipping his hot chocolate. "But I do know that you shouldn't assume stuff about people. You should communicate with them and give them a chance to tell you what they think."

Peiling's attention was distracted by the sight of a familiar-looking figure skating jerkily at the far end of the rink.

"Look—I think that's my teacher," she said, recognizing the brown velvet coat. "Don't you think she's pretty?" she added, pointing.

He squinted in the darkness. "I can't really see her from here."

Peiling rose to her feet, wanting to skate over. "Let's go over and say hi." Then she stopped herself. "Well, I'm not sure now's a good time." Miss Rosenweig was staggering across the ice in an attempt to regain her balance after tripping.

"I see what you mean," Uncle Samson said, standing

up also. Miss Rosenweig had ended her wild career face-down on the ice. He sat back down. "But I've got to give it to her . . ."

"What?" Peiling said.

"She's not afraid of falling. And you know what they say . . ."

"What?"

"*Bu ru huxue, yan de huzi*," he mumbled in Chinese.

"What did you say?"

"It means, 'If you don't enter the tiger's den, how do you catch a tiger cub?'"

Peiling shook her head. "What does that have to do with ice-skating?"

"It means you have to take chances to get any-where. Like when you're ice-skating, you'll learn a lot faster if you're not afraid to fall." He laughed a little. "At least, that's what your mom used to say, when we were kids. Somebody—one of our rich cousins, I can't remember who—gave us an old bike. It could barely hold together. Its handlebars were crooked, and its wheels wobbled."

Peiling was silent. It was always hard for her to imagine that Mama and Uncle Samson had been so poor in Taiwan that they couldn't even afford a bike.

Uncle Samson continued, "All of us, Aunt Yanyan, your mother, Uncle Paul, and I, tried to learn. We kept on falling down. But your mother would never give up. She was always the bravest of us."

"Really?" Peiling said dubiously.

"Yup. Eventually she was the first one to learn, and then she taught me to ride that darn thing."

Peiling didn't say anything. Mama always seemed so nervous and easily upset to her. It was hard for Peiling to think of her as brave.

At the other end of the rink, Miss Rosenweig had gotten to her feet and straightened her hat. In silence, they watched her make her wobbly way around the far curve.

"Maybe I'll get to meet your teacher some other time," Uncle Samson said.

He finished his hot chocolate, the last slurp reverberating hollowly in the bottom of the styrofoam cup. "It's getting late, Peiling," he said. "Time to go home."

6

When they walked in the side door of the Wang house, the first thing Mama said to Uncle Samson was, "What'd you do to your hair? Your—what do you call them—" She drew her index finger down the side of her cheekbone. "Your sideburns are too long. Caterpillars. They look like caterpillars."

"Keanu Reeves has his hair cut like this."

"Keanu Reeves doesn't have big ears."

So much for communication, Peiling thought, as she took off her coat and her shoes.

Baba was whacking a chicken into bite-size pieces with an enormous cleaver. He was wearing a plastic-coated apron to protect his work clothes. Mama scooped the rice while Baba brought the chicken over to the table. A platter of fish and one of bok choy were already steaming on the table. Peiling laid out four pairs of chopsticks and carried over four bowls of watercress soup.

Everyone sat down to eat. The grown-ups started talking about the elections in Taiwan, and a new kind of antiwrinkle cream Mama's company was bringing out.

Peiling shoveled rice into her mouth, hardly listening. She was still thinking about Uncle Samson's advice. All the other aunties and uncles were always laughing at his opinions, but you had to give it to him, he was a logical guy. He would calmly fix Baba's computer while Baba was grinding his teeth and swearing in Taiwanese over his shoulder. Maybe Uncle Samson was right, and she should just ask Mama and Baba about Christmas.

She leapt at the first break in the conversation, afraid that she'd chicken out if she waited too long. She cleared her throat. "Mama, Baba," she blurted, so loudly that everyone jumped. She tried again in a softer voice, "Mama, Baba . . ."

"Yes, Peiling?"

She took a deep breath. "Can we celebrate Christmas this year?"

Mama and Baba looked at one another, their chopsticks loaded with food stopping in midair.

Baba pulled a long face. "Christmas is an American holiday."

"*I'm* American," Peiling said.

"You're American, too," Uncle Samson reminded Baba. "You and Shuli became citizens five years ago."

Baba looked surprised and offended. "I may be a U.S. citizen but I'm not American," he said stiffly. It was true; he never really seemed to consider himself American.

Two years ago when a Taiwanese Ping-Pong player won an Olympic medal, he had leapt from his chair with tears in his eyes. It hadn't mattered to him how many dozens of medals the Americans had won.

"Yes, now we live here in the States," he told Uncle Samson in Chinese. "But I don't forget I was raised in a different culture. We don't want Peiling to forget either. That's why we celebrate Chinese holidays and make her learn Chinese."

"You could celebrate the Chinese holidays *and* celebrate Christmas," Uncle Samson suggested, switching back to English. "It's not a logical impossibility, you know."

"We could," Baba said. "But why would we?"

Peiling felt daunted, but Uncle Samson was nodding at her encouragingly. Beneath the table, she twisted and kneaded her napkin between sweating fingers. "I think it would be fun," she said.

"Fun! What would be fun about it?" Baba stared at her in genuine amazement.

"Everything." Her tongue, dry and clumsy, seemed to stick in her throat, but she forced herself to stumble on. "We could have a tree, and stockings hanging on the fireplace, and Santa—"

"Santa!" snorted Baba. "A fat old man in a red suit giving spoiled American children toys with enough electronic parts to power a supercomputer . . ."

Peiling felt herself wilting under the open contempt in Baba's voice. Of course she should have known how it would be. Why did he make her feel bad for wanting things just because he didn't want them? She should never have let Uncle Samson convince her. She slumped in her chair, staring down at her bowl of rice.

"But I think it would be fun too," she heard Mama say slowly.

Peiling looked up, her heart beating with a wild hope.

"What?" Baba said, as startled as she was.

"I said, I think it would be fun to celebrate Christmas," Mama repeated.

Baba stared at her. "But Christmas is a Christian holiday!"

"So?" Mama waved her chopsticks in dismissal. "Everyone knows that you don't have to be Christian to celebrate Christmas. Ever heard of a Hanukkah bush?" Peiling had, but didn't know that Mama had.

Apparently Baba hadn't. He said explosively, "We have our own traditions, our own holidays, and you want to—"

Mama interrupted him. "No one ever said anything about giving up our own traditions. What's the problem with celebrating Christmas for once?" She took a bite from her chicken wing and chewed it. "Live a little."

Baba lost his temper. He slapped his chopsticks down onto the table with a snap. "The problem," he shouted, "is that when we go back to Taiwan to visit Agong and Ama when Peiling's older, I want them to see their granddaughter, not some stranger with pimples and a pierced tongue!" According to Baba, Taiwanese kids didn't get pimples when they were teenagers because they didn't eat greasy American junk food.

"Taiwanese kids pierce their tongues, too," Peiling muttered rebelliously.

Baba turned on her sharply. His face was nearly purple, and his eyes were popping. "That's beside the point," he snapped. "The point is—" He suddenly stopped himself.

His gaze went to his right hand, clenched into a tight, white-knuckled fist on the table. Looking at his hand, he took a deep, slow breath and deliberately relaxed his fingers. Even though Baba was not even forty, he had high blood pressure. The doctor always said he'd die of a heart attack one of these days if he didn't learn how to control his temper.

Mama refilled his bowl of soup without saying a word. Baba drank it, breathing slowly between each sip.

Uncle Samson said to Baba in Taiwanese, "You don't have to be so strict with Peiling. She's only a kid."

Before Baba could respond, Mama retorted sharply in the same language, "Don't talk to your elders like that."

Baba picked up his chopsticks and began to eat again. Uncle Samson looked at Mama from under his brows for a moment. Then he, too, began to eat.

There was a strained silence. Peiling put her chopsticks down. She watched the sprigs of watercress floating sluggishly in her soup.

Mama broke the silence. "Peiling, you haven't eaten

anything." She pinched a plump chicken drumstick with her chopsticks and put it in Peiling's bowl.

"Did I tell you that there's a new girl in product development at work?" Mama continued brightly, trying to change the subject. "She's from Taiwan, too, and very pretty. Her name is Fang Lili . . ."

7

When Peiling got off the bus with the other girls at Laura's house, huge, fluffy flakes of snow had just started drifting down from the sky. As Laura and Grace, then Emma and Britney ran giggling up the walk, Peiling trailed behind. This was the closest she'd ever get to celebrating Christmas, she told herself: tagging along at Laura Hamilton's cookie-baking party. It was like looking in the window of a candy store when you didn't have any money. No, it was more like watching someone else open presents when you hadn't gotten anything yourself.

The moment that Laura pushed open the front door, however, Peiling's gloomy thoughts vanished. The rich, buttery aromas of something baking rushed out and enveloped her. She walked in through the front door with its stained glass panels, cautiously wiping her feet on the monogrammed doormat. The house looked like a picture from a magazine, all dark wood and big, plush furniture. From somewhere upstairs, a man's voice on the stereo crooned:

I'm dreaming of a white Christmas
Just like the ones I used to know . . .

Through an arched doorway, Peiling caught a glimpse of a Christmas tree, glittering with silver tinsel and crystal ornaments, the golden star atop it nearly brushing the high ceiling. Peiling gazed at it hungrily. It was simply perfect.

On a side table was a cut-glass bowl of candy canes. Before she had even taken off her coat, Laura had helped herself to one and was offering them to Peiling. Sucking on her candy, Laura led everyone to the kitchen. Peiling tore herself away from the tree to catch up with the others.

In the kitchen, Mrs. Hamilton, who was willowy and blonde, was just taking loaves of golden, cranberry-studded nut bread out of the oven.

"Just a moment, girls." She took off her oven mitt and opened a laptop on the counter. "I need to send a quick e-mail to my office before we start on the cookies."

"Mom's the PR director for the Museum of Modern Art," Laura explained.

"Hey, what's that?" said Grace curiously, pointing at the computer. The screen showed a young woman in safety goggles and torn jeans. It looked like she was using a blowtorch to weld beer cans to a blackened car engine.

"Oh, that's a story on our Web site about some artists in the Warehouse District who make sculpture out of 'found objects.' You know, things that other people throw out, like beer cans," Mrs. Hamilton replied. She quickly typed out a short e-mail, and shut the laptop.

Laura introduced Peiling, who was the only one who had never been there before, to her mother.

"Nice to meet you, Peiling," Mrs. Hamilton said. "Are you ready to cut out the cookies, girls? Wash your hands first, don't forget."

As Mrs. Hamilton rolled out the cookie dough on the marble counter, the girls punched out wreaths and snowmen, Santas and reindeer. As they worked, the girls chattered about what they each wanted for Christmas. Only Peiling didn't say anything.

"What do you do for Christmas, Peiling?" said Mrs. Hamilton, putting a pan of cookies into the oven.

"Peiling doesn't celebrate Christmas, Mom," Laura put in importantly.

"Oh, really?" Mrs. Hamilton said in surprise. "What do you do instead?"

"Nothing much, really," Peiling said, embarrassed. "Last year my parents used Christmas vacation to retile the bathroom. On Christmas Day my mother makes a big dinner, but it's just Chinese food like we eat every day."

"Chinese food?" said Mrs. Hamilton. "We love Chinese food. We just love the noodles at the Sun Luck Gardens. What do you think of their food?"

"I've never been there. My father says they make Chinese food for Americans, not for Chinese," Peiling replied uncomfortably. She knew it wasn't very polite, but she couldn't think of anything to say besides the truth.

Mrs. Hamilton didn't ask Peiling any more questions after that.

Now trays of cookies, crisp and golden brown around the edges, were coming out of the oven. Mrs. Hamilton took out bowls of fluffy white frosting. She gave the girls squeeze bottles of different shades of food coloring. "Just a drop or two, now," she warned.

Peiling watched in fascination as the drops of brilliant color swirled into and streaked the whiteness, before tinting the icing in each bowl a different delectable hue: rose pink, lemon yellow, or robin's-egg blue. Then Mrs. Hamilton set out icing pens and shakers full of rainbow sprinkles and colored sugars.

"Oooooh, my favorite part!" exclaimed Laura, grabbing a spatula.

Peiling started on a wreath. As she spread a thick layer of lime green frosting on the cookie, a gob of it fell on her hand. She licked it off.

"Oh, it tastes like almonds," she said in surprise.

"Yes, it's an old family recipe," said Mrs. Hamilton. She nodded at a thick scrapbook open on the counter. "I can give you the recipe if you like."

Mama almost never used recipes. She cooked by feel, she said, tasting and adding ingredients as she went along. Peiling looked at the Hamiltons' scrapbook with a feeling of awe. The edges of the pages were yellow with age. The recipe was handwritten in an old-fashioned, curlicued script.

At last all the cookies were frosted and decorated. Munching on the broken leg of a reindeer, Laura said to her mother, "Can I show Peiling the carousel?"

"Of course," Mrs. Hamilton nodded. Laura proudly led everyone upstairs to her parents' room. It was dominated by an enormous canopied bed with a dark-blue flowered bedspread and ruffled pillows. Mrs. Hamilton followed with a box of matches.

"Look at this," said Laura. She took a gleaming golden contraption down from a shelf. "Great-grandma gave this to Mom when she was a little girl. We light it when we open presents on Christmas Day."

Five candles stood around a circular base. Above the candles was a troupe of cutout angels blowing horns; and above them, a golden wheel with slanting blades like a propeller. Mrs. Hamilton lit the candles, and, like magic, the angels began to spin. The chimes hanging from their bodies struck against little silver bells, and all at once the room was filled with flickering shadows and tinkling music.

"The hot air from the candles rises and makes the wheel turn . . . ," Mrs. Hamilton explained, but Peiling wasn't listening.

She felt a sudden pang of pain. Everything fit together here like a beautiful puzzle. "White Christmas" on the stereo, and the snow outside. The Hamiltons' tree, and the tree in the town square. Their cookies, in pretty shapes frosted with colored sugars, and the pictures of cookies on the covers of magazines. Inside and outside echoed each other harmoniously, not like the Wang family, where everything that went on inside the house seemed totally disconnected from the outside world, a lonely island.

Choking down the lump in her throat, Peiling followed Laura and the other girls back to the kitchen. Over the music, she heard the unmistakable clank of Baba's muffler in the driveway.

Peiling ran to the front door, throwing on her coat. Mrs. Hamilton had already opened it. Baba was standing there in his tweed hat and overcoat, covered with snow.

"You must be Mr. Wang," said Mrs. Hamilton, beaming. "Why don't you come in and have a cup of coffee?"

"No, no!" Baba said, shaking his head and waving his hands as vigorously as if Mrs. Hamilton had just suggested that he dive into the icy pond next door. "No, thank you. Peiling's mother will have dinner waiting for us at home," he explained.

"Well, at least come in and try a cookie. The girls have been working on them all afternoon. Come in," Mrs. Hamilton repeated encouragingly, as he hesitated on the threshold. At last Baba stepped cautiously into the front hall, after stamping his feet on the doormat to knock the snow off his shoes.

Mrs. Hamilton bustled away and returned with a red-and-white frosted Santa in a napkin.

Baba took a bite.

"How do you like them? Didn't the girls do a wonderful job?"

"Excellent," said Baba, chewing and smiling broadly. But Peiling noticed that he had wrapped the rest of the cookie up in the napkin. "Thank you very much."

"You're quite welcome," Mrs. Hamilton said. "Well, come again soon, Peiling. You too, Mr. Wang."

Peiling said thank you to Mrs. Hamilton and goodbye to the girls. Then she followed Baba out to the car through the ankle-deep snow.

8

Dinner was a silent meal.

"How was Laura's?" Mama asked.

"Fine," was all that Peiling would allow herself to say. She was afraid that if she talked about her visit to the Hamiltons', the lingering feeling of enchantment would slip away.

Mama didn't say anything else. She seemed tired after her long day at work. Baba seemed moody, silently slurping his bowl of soup noodles.

After dinner was cleared, the three of them moved wordlessly to the family room. As usual, Peiling sat between Mama and Baba on the sofa. Baba turned on the local news.

"With just nineteen more shopping days left until Christmas, business is booming as customers in search of that perfect gift pack local stores," a perky newswoman reported from the mall.

Baba shook his head disgustedly as the TV showed shots of overfilled parking lots and long lines of waiting customers. "This proves my point," he said, as if winning an argument. "American culture is so materialistic."

Peiling couldn't help it. She felt sudden tears stinging her eyes. Before she could brush them away, she saw that Mama was looking at her.

Mama grabbed the remote control from the coffee table and clicked off the TV. "I say we celebrate Christmas," she said.

Baba looked from the blank TV screen to Mama, blinking.

"Remember, Wenzhe?" Mama went on. "We came here so Peiling could have opportunities we didn't. So don't act like you're still in Taiwan."

"I thought we went through this already." Baba attempted to straighten himself on the sagging cushions of the couch.

"Maybe you did, but I didn't," Mama retorted. "We've been here seven years. You can't expect Peiling not to want to do the things the other kids are doing."

"Exactly, the things the other children are doing!" Baba shot back. "Boyfriends at thirteen, drugs at fourteen, pregnant at fifteen—"

"Shhh, don't put ideas in her head," Mama hissed in Taiwanese.

"I? I put ideas in her head?" Baba sputtered. "You're the one who's encouraging her . . ."

Peiling ran up the dark stairs to her bedroom. She slammed the door. She threw herself on the bed. Even through the shut door, she could hear Mama and Baba downstairs. They had switched to Taiwanese, and their voices were getting louder and louder, angrier and angrier.

She flicked on the light. Her hands shaking, she took out the Captain America comic book that Grace had lent her, and tried to concentrate on it through her tears. Captain America, his red, white, and blue shield in hand, was trying to defuse the bomb-loaded drone plane launched by an evil Nazi scientist . . .

She was on the last page when she heard steps on the stairs.

Baba came in.

"What are you reading, Peiling?"

She showed him the cover, afraid she would burst into tears if she tried to speak.

"Captain America," he read. He looked at the picture of the muscle-bound superhero in a star-spangled bodysuit. He shook his head. "Can you imagine any self-respecting Taiwanese man walking around in a getup like that—" He cut himself off, as if remembering what Mama had coached him not to say.

After a moment, he asked, "Do you know how to say 'America' in Chinese?"

Peiling shook her head.

He took a pencil and swiftly wrote two characters on a sheet of paper. "It's *Meiguo*, 'beautiful country,' because when the first Chinese came here they thought it was the most beautiful place they had ever seen. Do you know how to say 'China' in Chinese?"

"*Zhongguo*?" Peiling managed to say.

"Do you know what the characters for *Zhongguo* are?" Baba wrote two more characters on the sheet. "This means 'central' or 'middle country,' because from the very beginning the Chinese thought that their country was the center of the civilized world."

Baba put the pencil down and sighed. "How old were you when we left Taiwan?"

"Three."

"Do you remember anything about it?"

"No," Peiling shook her head. "Yes," she corrected herself suddenly. "The fried oyster pancakes."

Baba's face lit up. "The fried oyster pancakes. *Ou-a jian.*" He said the Taiwanese name. "We would bike to the night market, and have them there. We've never found a place that knew how to make them here. Do you know how to write 'oyster'?" He scribbled another character on the paper. "That's a hard character."

He put the pencil down. "So what exactly do you want to do for Christmas?" he said quietly.

Peiling looked up quickly, eagerly. She knew she was disappointing him, but she couldn't help herself. "I want a real American Christmas," she blurted. "With a tree and American food, turkey with stuffing."

Baba sighed again as he tried to smile. "All right, let's go downstairs and see what Mama says."

Peiling raced down to the kitchen. She heard Baba's footsteps plodding heavily down the stairs behind her. To her surprise, Uncle Samson was there with Mama. He must have come over while she and Baba had been talking upstairs. Peiling guessed that he had caved in to pressure from Mama, for he was letting her doctor his sideburns. He was sitting on a kitchen chair on an island of spread-out newspaper. A pair of electric clippers buzzed menacingly in Mama's right hand, while her left hand held a black plastic comb.

"We're celebrating Christmas," Baba said curtly.

Mama switched off the clippers. She nodded briskly, as if she weren't surprised. "I'll make a turkey, and we'll invite all the aunties and uncles. Everyone can bring an American dish," she promised.

"I'll pick up a tree on the way home from work Christmas Eve," Baba said. He went to the family room and buried his nose in a Chinese newspaper.

"How about one of those Douglas firs? I love the way they smell," Mama suggested.

Baba grunted without taking his head out of the paper.

Smiling, Mama held up a mirror so Uncle Samson could see her handiwork. "So, what do you think? A lot better, eh? I hope Fang Lili likes it," she said.

Uncle Samson ignored her. He caught Peiling's eye in the mirror. He looked simply awful, with bits of hair stuck to his face and his shoulders covered by a cape of shiny pink polyester fastened with a wooden clothespin. He tried to wink at her, but he couldn't close only one eye without scrunching up his whole face.

Peiling understood what he meant anyway and grinned back.

9

A string of nasal beeps sounded beside Peiling's ear. She blinked, groping blindly for the alarm clock, and slapped the off button down. She rubbed her eyes. Around the edge of the roll-down blind, she could see the cold, gray light of an early winter's morning.

Then she remembered: they were going to have Christmas! She flopped back down against the pillows and shut her eyes again. For a few minutes, she lay there luxuriating in the sense of happy anticipation that filled her. Then she jumped out of bed and checked the "to do" list she had made last night on a blank page at the back of her math notebook.

There were fourteen items on the list. The first item was "Learn Christmas songs," followed by a list of seven or eight of her favorite carols. Number one was, of course, "Chestnuts roasting on an open fire . . ." Item two was "Presents." Beneath it, she had written, "Uncle Samson: Hair gel? Grace: NASA poster? . . ." And so it continued until the last item on the list, "House decorations: holly, candles, wreath, mistletoe."

She thought for a moment, and then added the words "inflatable Santa" to the last item. She had seen an inflatable Santa in a store display, and was unable to resist the vision of it waving merrily beside the front door. She could never convince Mama to buy one, so she resolved to spend what remained of last year's Chinese New Year money on it.

"Peiling! Breakfast!" Mama's voice floated up from downstairs.

Peiling threw open her closet. She chose a pair of bright red corduroy pants and a green sweater, and dashed downstairs.

"And Christmas tree ornaments. We'll need Christmas tree ornaments," Peiling told Mama.

Mama's eyes were on the rearview mirror. Her ungloved knuckles gleamed white on the steering wheel as she wove through the morning rush-hour traffic. "Crazy old bat. Do you need glasses?" Mama muttered as a battered Oldsmobile cut her off.

"Did you hear me?" Peiling asked.

"Yes, yes. Christmas tree ornaments." Mama rolled down the window and stuck her head and arm out so someone would let her into the turn lane in front of Peiling's school.

"Tinsel. Silver, not gold," Peiling said.

"Silver tinsel." With a screech of the tires, Mama made the turn.

"Lights, all different colors."

"Colored lights." Mama pulled up in front of the door next to the auditorium.

"Glass ornaments. Which do you think is nicer, round or bell-shaped?" Peiling said, climbing out of the car.

"Round."

"Well, but bell-shaped is nice, too. How about some of each? Do you need me to write this down for you?" Peiling called from the sidewalk.

Mama was already pulling away from the curb.

Peiling walked into Drama Club, pondering whether or not that spray-on fake snow was too tacky. She was unpleasantly surprised by the sight of Simon Pence, already dressed as the pauper, in the middle of the stage surrounded by a large group. Through the ragged holes in his costume, he was showing everyone the scabs that encrusted his legs and arms.

"What are those from?" Peiling asked.

"Chicken pox," Simon said proudly. "They thought it was Rocky Mountain spotted fever at first, but it turned out to be just plain old chicken pox."

Peiling found herself wishing that it had been Rocky Mountain spotted fever. "Are you sure you're not still contagious?" she asked sourly. She was pleased when the other kids backed away from him.

Laura came in, staggering under the weight of a stack of books. She didn't even look at Peiling, much less say hi.

"I've been doing some research," she announced. "A lot of things we're doing aren't as accurate as they should be." She walked over to Madeline, and plucked at her costume. "Look," she said accusingly. "Leg-of-mutton sleeves. These didn't even come into fashion until the eighteenth century."

Madeline started to cry.

Now that Simon had returned, it was back to props for Peiling. Trying to shake off her disappointment, she left the stage and got out the glue gun. She dragged out the old dining room chair that she had spray-painted gold two weeks ago. She began to attach bits of colored glass to it. It would be Laura's throne. Maybe Laura would sit in it when she needed a break from ordering everyone around.

From the stage she heard Simon declaim, "I live in da city, please thee, Your Highness. Offal Court, off Pudding Lane."

"Mrs. Baldino," came an anguished shriek from Laura. "Make him stop! He keeps saying 'da' instead of 'the.'"

"Why shouldn't I?" demanded Simon. "My man Tom's a homeboy from the 'hood." Only he said "da 'hood" instead of "the 'hood."

All through the rehearsal, Peiling kept hearing Laura's shrill voice complaining about Simon's performance. Did Mrs. Baldino really think it was a good idea for Simon to slouch and put his hands in his pockets when he spoke his lines? Finally, Simon swallowed his words so Laura could hardly understand them.

No, Peiling certainly didn't envy Simon, having to work so closely with Laura. But at the end of rehearsal, when she was scrubbing glue off her hands, Laura came up to her.

"Here, Peiling," Laura said, a little shyly, handing her a small box. "These are some of the cookies we made on Friday. I forgot to give you some to take home."

Peiling was surprised at Laura's thoughtfulness. "Thanks," she said, opening the box and peeking inside. Beneath the billows of tissue paper was a selection of the most beautifully decorated cookies, one of each shape. She couldn't resist adding nonchalantly, "Actually, we'll be making cookies at my house, too. We're celebrating Christmas this year."

"Really?" Laura sniffed. Instead of looking suitably impressed, she looked skeptical.

"Yes, really." There was something about the way Laura looked at her that always made Peiling feel like Laura was secretly criticizing her. That was why Peiling always ended up losing her temper with Laura. "It'll be a real American Christmas, with a tree, and decorations, and a turkey—," Peiling began hotly.

"Peiling, could I talk to you for a moment?" Mrs. Baldino interrupted, putting her hand on Peiling's shoulder. Eyeing Laura with the look of a hunted rabbit, she waited until Laura had reluctantly moved away.

Mrs. Baldino drew Peiling aside to the cluttered janitor's closet that doubled as a prop room.

She shut the door. "I want you to learn the pauper's part," she whispered conspiratorially.

Peiling was surprised. "But Mrs. Baldino, Simon's better now, and he'll be able to do it—," she began.

Mrs. Baldino shook her head vigorously. "That doesn't matter. He could get sick again. You never know what's going to happen."

"But it'll take me ages to learn the part," Peiling excused herself. "And it will probably all just go to waste."

"You know what the Boy Scouts say. "*Estote parati.*"

Peiling had no idea what Mrs. Baldino was talking about.

"Be prepared," Mrs. Baldino explained. "It's Latin. Better safe than sorry."

But Peiling persisted in demurring. "And I'm going to be very busy, you know, getting ready for Christmas."

"Christmas!" Mrs. Baldino exclaimed impatiently. "What does Christmas have to do with anything?"

She stared at Peiling, jerking herself upright to her full height of five feet two, as if Peiling had somehow insulted her. "Frankly, Peiling, I'm baffled by your attitude. It's a wonderful chance for you to play the pauper. Don't you want to?"

Somehow, Mrs. Baldino's question pulled Peiling up short. "I . . . I . . . ," she stammered, confused. Why had she been so busy telling herself what a relief it was not to have to work with Laura? Was it to hide her own disappointment that Simon, and not she, would be playing the pauper?

She realized with a sudden jolt that she was tired of always being backstage, behind the scenes, invisibly supporting those in front. This time she wanted to be onstage. She wanted to speak lines, and feel all the eyes on her. It came to her, all at once, that she hated Laura so much in part because she envied her. Laura occupied center stage effortlessly, and demanded to be the center of attention as naturally as she breathed.

"Yes," Peiling told Mrs. Baldino slowly. "Yes, I did want to play the part, but—"

"Of course you did," Mrs. Baldino said. She nodded as if she had known all along. "You did, because playing the part helps you express a part of yourself." She took Peiling's shoulders. Behind the lenses of her bifocals, her watery blue eyes, still piercing under their hood of wrinkles, looked into Peiling's. "You mustn't be afraid of that."

"Besides," she continued. "Now that I've seen you read, I wish you had tried out for the pauper." She glanced around furtively even though no one was around. "I don't care what Laura thinks, it's not about how you look, it's all about how you *feel* for a character. Simon Pence isn't going to make anyone believe that he's ever felt lonely or hungry for a day in his life."

"Now," Mrs. Baldino went on briskly. "If you spend

half an hour a night, you'll know the part by the end of December."

Peiling thought of the list at the back of her notebook. "Well, maybe. If I have the time . . ."

"No maybes." Mrs. Baldino shook her head decidedly. "Don't say maybe, say yes, because I know you're the kind of person who means what she says. Now promise me, half an hour each night."

"Ummm," Peiling didn't understand how Mrs. Baldino could know any such thing about her. She looked down, but Mrs. Baldino caught her by the chin and held Peiling's shrinking gaze with her own. "Promise," Mrs. Baldino said commandingly.

Peiling had never realized that nervous, easily flustered Mrs. Baldino could be so forceful. "Oh, all right," said Peiling. "I promise."

Satisfied, Mrs. Baldino unzipped Peiling's backpack and stuffed her own copy of the script inside.

10

It was the twenty-third of December, the last day of school before Christmas vacation. Peiling and Grace knelt beside Miss Rosenweig pasting the last few magazine clippings onto the collage. Then the three of them stepped back to look at their handiwork.

Every inch of the five-foot-square plywood board was covered with photos cut out from newspapers and magazines, of everything from Australian bushmen to Zulu chieftains. There were Balinese dancers, Sami reindeer herders, Mongolian yurts. The kids had cut them out and pasted them on as neatly as they could, but somehow the whole effect looked messy and amateurish. The corners of some pictures curled up; the surfaces of others were grotesquely bubbled with blobs of glue.

Peiling looked at Grace. Grace shook her head grimly, looking at Miss Rosenweig, but didn't say anything.

"Bring the pasta over, please," Miss Rosenweig said. Laura and Sandra, who had been using food coloring to dye different pasta shapes, came over from the other side of the room with paper-towel covered trays of corkscrews, bowties, and elbow macaroni. Even though the shapes had been dyed in different shades of food coloring, for some reason they had all come out almost the same dingy gray. Over her tray of bowties, Laura's face wore a sour "I told you so" expression.

"Let's see . . . ," Miss Rosenweig said. She held a few pieces of elbow macaroni against the background of magazine clippings, and tilted her head critically to observe the effect. "Hmmm," she said dubiously.

It was the fulfillment of Peiling's worst nightmare. The color of the pasta was so dull it blended in with the clippings. It looked like a bunch of random stuff from the garbage had been glued onto the plywood by a classroom of blindfolded kindergartners.

"Talk about 'found objects,' " Laura muttered.

At that moment Mr. Guy walked in. He took one look at the collage and said, "Oh my God, Deanna. Why didn't you tell me?"

"Tell you what?"

"That you were having so much trouble with your project. Look, we can download some images from the Web and blow them up. It's really easy. I'll show you how."

"I don't want to download some images from the Web," Miss Rosenweig said stubbornly. "I want to do a collage."

"Well, okay. So you want to do a collage, but then

you need some sort of simple, recognizable shape to pull it together. Like how about a nice Christmas tree . . ."

"I don't want a Christmas tree." Miss Rosenweig looked mulish. "I want a chicken."

Mr. Guy blinked. "A chicken? Look, Deanna, I know you're always trying to do your own thing, but a chicken?"

Miss Rosenweig cut him off. "Don't you think you'd better get back to your own class?"

Mr. Guy left, looking huffy. But after he was gone Laura said, "Maybe Mr. Guy's right."

Sandra nodded emphatically.

"Yeah, I mean, it's not too late. Maybe we could do something else," Laura continued. "Like, we could sing 'Joy to the World.' I know a really fantastic arrangement, with a soprano solo, which I'd be more than happy to do—"

"Yeah," Steven said eagerly. "Or, we could do a Christmas rap. I could bring my beat box and lay some grooves . . ."

Miss Rosenweig's face fell. "I thought you guys liked the collage," she said.

Bewildered, Peiling took in her teacher's slumped shoulders and quivering lips. Miss Rosenweig always seemed so cheerful and spunky that Peiling could never have imagined her discouraged. A picture of Miss Rosenweig teetering precariously around the ice-skating rink flashed into her mind. Suddenly Peiling felt sorry for her.

"I think the collage is a good idea," Peiling found herself saying.

To Peiling's intense relief, Grace piped up also. "Actually, I think it's a good idea, too." Grace plucked a gray bowtie from the tray and began to pace up and down the classroom, clutching it in her hand. "The problem is the medium. Macaroni is the wrong medium," she said.

"What's a medium?" asked Steven.

"It's in between a large and a small, you idiot," said Laura.

"That's not how we talk to each other in this class," said Miss Rosenweig sharply. She seemed to be snapping back to her usual self a bit. "And actually, a medium is the materials you use to make art, for example, watercolors or pastels or clay or marble." She was looking at Grace with a hopeful expression dawning in her eyes. "And the medium is very important. In fact, it can totally transform the impact of a work of art . . ."

Grace tossed the bowtie back onto the tray. "You need to make the foreground jump out from the background. You need higher contrast. And as for the background, the clippings don't work. They're too small, and too distracting. Mr. Guy is right. You need a clear, recognizable symbol."

Miss Rosenweig nodded, staring at Grace. "Like a globe," she said slowly.

"Or a map of the world," Peiling suggested.

"A map of the world," Miss Rosenweig echoed. "That's perfect!"

At that moment the afternoon bell rang. It was the official beginning of Christmas vacation. A joyful roar filled the classroom as everyone scrambled for their coats and bookbags.

"Class dismissed!" Miss Rosenweig said. Her "Happy Hanukkah!" was drowned out by a chorus of Merry Christmases. Only Grace remained standing stock-still, sketching something in her notebook as the others jostled by her.

Peiling squeezed through the crowds to get her backpack and down jacket. She threw on the jacket and opened her desk. Carefully, she took out the presents she had made in art class. For Baba, she had traced the shape of Taiwan onto a slab of wood and hammered nails all around the outline. Then she had wound green thread around and between the nails until the shape of the island was all filled in. For Mama, there was an apron silk-screened with the words, "Don't mess with THE COOK."

The last thing she took out of her desk was a small box of Christmas cookies. On the way out to the bus, she ran to catch up with Laura Hamilton.

"Here," she said, thrusting the box at Laura. "I wanted to give you these in return."

Peiling swelled with pride as Laura opened the box to reveal the Christmas cookies that Mama had helped her bake. Mama had turned out to be a good baker. There were sleds, candy canes, and Christmas trees, crisp and golden and frosted in bright colors, carefully wrapped in aluminum foil.

"Thanks. They look good," Laura said, smiling. "Well, have a good Christmas!"

"I will," Peiling said, running for her bus. "Merry Christmas to you too!"

On Christmas Eve, Peiling padded downstairs in her pajamas to make sure that everything was ready for the next day. In the living room, a red and white striped kneesock, which she had ironed the day before, was tacked over the fireplace. A small sprig of mistletoe dangled over the arched entrance of the living room.

Peiling went to the front hall. She opened the front door and stuck her head out into the chilly night air. A holly wreath glistening with plump red berries hung on the door. On the porch, the Santa, which she had blown up with a bicycle pump that afternoon, was floating peacefully on its tether. She pulled her head in and shut the door.

From the garage came the sound of Baba's electric drill. Peiling put on her coat over her pajamas and shuffled out to the garage in her slippers. The Christmas tree was still on top of Baba's car, looking like a prisoner with its branches lashed helplessly to its trunk. Baba, bending over his workbench in safety goggles, was making a stand for the tree out of an old coffee can. The drill whined as he bored another hole into the side of the can. He saw her and turned off the drill. She went over.

"Hold the can," he told her. She held it while he used wing nuts to attach the three metal legs. Then he took the can from her and placed it on the cement floor of the garage. It wobbled a little when he nudged it.

"Look," he said, showing her. "One of the legs is a tiny bit higher than the others. I'll have to redrill the hole." He unscrewed the leg. He showed her a piece of red flannel with stars on it that she recognized as one of her old pajamas. "And I'll cover the can with this afterwards so it will look prettier," he added gruffly.

As he demonstrated how he would attach the flannel to the can with Velcro fastenings, Peiling understood that even though he hadn't wanted to celebrate Christmas in the first place, he was determined to do a thorough job of it. Suddenly she felt like giving him a hug, even though they almost never hugged in the Wang family. However, he had already turned the drill on again. She went back inside from the garage.

"Time for bed," Mama said. She was curled up on the sofa in the family room, poring over the magazine Peiling had bought her from the checkout counter in the supermarket. *Ham Like You've Never Had It; Turkey Three Ways;* and *Old Favorites and New Traditions,* its cover promised.

Peiling went upstairs. With a sigh, she sat down at her

desk and opened *The Prince and the Pauper*, as she had promised Mrs. Baldino. She had all but the last act memorized. She turned to the last few pages of the script. The old king had died, and the pauper Tom Canty was about to be crowned the new King of England. Just as he was about to be declared king, a boy dressed in tatters burst into Westminster Abbey. It was the real Prince Edward. At once the guards tried to throw the ragged intruder out. "Seize the vagabond!"

But then the pauper ran forward with a glad face to meet him, and fell on his knees before him. Peiling read the pauper's next line out loud. "O, my lord, the king. Let poor Tom Canty be first to swear fealty to thee and say, 'Put on thy crown and enter into thine own again!'"

Peiling reread the line, puzzling over it. Why would Tom Canty be so glad that the true prince had reappeared? Even if it were the right thing to do to surrender the throne, why would anyone prefer to be poor and hungry, rather than a prince? Wouldn't he have been disappointed when the prince showed up, instead of relieved and happy?

She shrugged impatiently. She couldn't be bothered with such questions now. Mechanically, she memorized the rest of the page, until she heard the clock downstairs strike.

Nine o'clock. Only three more hours until Christmas! Peiling shut the script. She stooped beside her bed. She bent down and counted the presents hidden beneath, knobby under their coverings of wrapping paper and Scotch tape. She went to her closet and chose an outfit for the next day, a red plaid dress and green tights. Finally she shut off the light and climbed under the covers.

For a long time she lay awake, imagining what Christmas would be like. She pictured the tree sparkling with tinsel and glass, and Baba's face lighting up with joy as he opened the gift she had made him. She heard Uncle Samson's rumbling voice harmonizing with Mama's quavering high one as they gathered around the piano to sing "Silent Night." With her eyes shut, she imagined biting into a succulent mouthful of turkey and stuffing smothered with gravy.

She was just drifting off to sleep when she heard the door to the garage open and Baba come in.

"It's started to snow," Baba said.

"Really?" Mama replied indifferently. "Then it's a good thing we got those snow tires put on last week."

Peiling jumped out of bed and ran to the window. In the light from the streetlamp she saw the flakes whirling down thick and fast. Already the mailbox glittered a ghostly white. The suburban street looked both beautiful and strangely alien. It looked like it would be a white Christmas after all. Peiling snuggled under her covers and fell asleep.

11

Even before she opened her eyes, Peiling knew. It was Christmas! She sprang out of bed and ran to open the shades. It was no longer snowing. The morning sun glittered everywhere on a thick layer of pure white snow, still untouched by the snowplows. Too excited to dress, she raced breathlessly downstairs in her pajamas and bare feet.

Baba was stooped in the corner of the living room straightening the Christmas tree in its coffee can holder. Freed from their constricting bonds, the lushly needled boughs sprang gracefully from the tall trunk, filling the air with their sweet scent. Its top nearly brushed the ceiling.

"It's beautiful!" Peiling cried.

"Where are your slippers? You'll catch cold," Baba said.

Peiling ignored him and ran to the fireplace. She yanked her bulging stocking down from the mantelpiece. Out tumbled candy, colored pencils, a bracelet of coral beads, and some new hair clips.

She popped a red-foil-wrapped chocolate kiss into her mouth, even though she hadn't had breakfast yet. She fastened the clips in her unbrushed hair. Suddenly, she noticed that there were a few dried plums in crinkled paper wrappings with Chinese writing on them, scattered amid the deluge of candy canes and chocolate kisses. Normally she loved to eat them, but today they seemed out of place. She stuffed them in her pocket.

Slipping the bracelet onto her wrist, she ran to the kitchen. Mama, in curlers and a bathrobe, was setting out three bowls of cold cereal. Mama usually served only hot breakfasts.

"Mmmm," said Peiling, grabbing her spoon and beginning to munch the sugar-coated flakes before they got soggy.

"It's because I have so much cooking to do today," Mama explained apologetically, tying on an apron over her bathrobe. "Can you decorate the tree this morning, and set the table after lunch? But get dressed first. You'll catch cold in your bare feet."

Peiling nodded, wolfing down her cereal. She went upstairs and dressed in the clothes she had put out the night before. Then she ran back down to the living room and joyfully opened the brand-new boxes of tinsel and lights and glass ornaments that Mama had bought.

Baba got out a stepladder from the garage. He climbed up and began to string the lights. Peiling dragged over a chair. She unwound the spools of silvery tinsel and draped them artistically over the tree. Then she began to hang the ornaments, tinkly glass balls and bells in gold and red and blue and green. She would climb up on the chair and hang two or three, and then scramble off to observe the effect. Up and down she went, until she was nearly dizzy, hanging more ornaments and making tiny adjustments to the ones she had already put up.

"Ready?" Baba asked, a little impatiently.

Peiling shifted a blue ball to a slightly higher branch, and then got off the chair. "Okay."

Baba plugged in the lights. The tree twinkled and sparkled, yet to Peiling it didn't look quite right.

"Something's missing," she muttered. Had she forgotten anything? Rapidly she ran over the list in her head: tinsel, ornaments, lights . . .

"A star," Baba said suddenly. "The Hamiltons had a star on top of theirs."

Peiling's jaw dropped. It came as news to her that Baba had even noticed that the Hamiltons had a tree. "But I forgot to ask Mama to get one," she said. She felt a wave of disappointment wash over her. "And I bet all the shops are closed today."

Baba looked at the tree, frowning. Then his face broke into a smile. "Don't worry. I have an idea."

He trundled to the hall closet where Mama kept rolls of wrapping paper and ribbons. He pulled out a roll of shiny golden paper, and found a yardstick and a pair of scissors. Peiling followed him to the kitchen table, where he cut six large squares from the wrapping paper. He smoothed one flat, and began to fold it into something like a rectangular envelope, with a flap and a pocket.

"What are you doing?" Mama said from the sink. She had changed out of her bathrobe and was wearing a blouse and pants now, but her hair was still in curlers. She was bent over a raw turkey, so enormous that it filled the whole kitchen sink. As Peiling watched, she stuck her rubber-gloved hand into its body and pulled out a handful of giblets.

"You'll see," Baba said, chuckling. He was folding another of the squares in the same way as the first one. "I used to do a lot of origami when I was a kid. Let's see if I still remember."

Mama stripped off the gloves and came over to the table. As she and Peiling watched, he folded the four remaining squares in the same way. Then he began to put the rectangles together, tucking the flap of one into the pocket of another. As if by magic, a three-dimensional twelve-pointed star took shape under his nimble fingers. As Peiling watched wonderingly, he pierced one point with a needle, and strung a gold ribbon through the hole. Peiling and Mama followed him back to the living room. He climbed the stepladder and fastened the star to the very top of the tree.

All three of them stepped back to look. The gold star was the perfect touch. Their tree was even more beautiful than the Hamiltons'. As Peiling looked at it, shimmering with tinsel and gold and lights, she felt as if she too were lit up from the inside by the same brightness.

"Pretty good, huh?" Baba said, nudging Mama with his elbow.

"Not so bad," Mama said. She pulled Baba over to the mistletoe hanging from the archway and kissed him. Peiling giggled. She didn't even know that Mama knew about mistletoe.

"What's that for?" Baba said, surprised.

Mama pointed up at the mistletoe.

"What's that?" he asked.

"It's mistletoe. You're supposed to kiss under the mistletoe."

"Why's that?"

Instead of answering, Mama kissed him again.

12

For lunch, Baba and Peiling stood at the kitchen counter eating cold leftovers. Mama, sitting at the table before a litter of cutting boards and vegetable scraps, didn't join them. Her face was plastered with a greenish mud facial mask and she couldn't eat, she said, without disturbing it. Instead she busily peeled potato after potato. Her face, covered with mud except for circles around the eyes and mouth, had a perpetually startled expression.

" 'On't eat 'oo much. 'Ave 'ome 'omach for 'inner," Mama reminded her. Peiling could hardly understand her, since she was trying to speak while moving her mouth as little as possible. " 'O set 'e 'able." After puzzling for a moment, Peiling realized that Mama had said, "Don't eat too much. Save some stomach for dinner. Go set the table."

Humming "O Christmas Tree," Peiling ran into the dining room. Mama had put out the fat bundle of ivory chopsticks that they used for special occasions. Peiling put them back in the drawer. She got out knives and forks and spoons instead. She polished the silver candle-sticks. She screwed new white candles into them, and put a box of matches beside them.

Then she remembered the wineglasses that someone had given Mama and Baba long ago as a wedding present. She climbed on a chair to get them down. She dusted them off and arranged them on the table too.

By this time the excitingly unfamiliar smell of turkey was wafting through the house. Peiling rushed into the kitchen, sniffing greedily, "How's the cooking going?"

"Fine," said Mama, busily peeling carrots. She had scrubbed off the facial mask and the curlers were out, leaving her chin-length hair much wavier and fuller than usual. She had put on lipstick and blush, and a wine-red dress. Although she still wore an apron, it was a fancy, ruffled one that she only wore when people were over. Instead of slippers, her shoes, a pair of burgundy pumps, clicked briskly on the linoleum. "The turkey's almost ready."

Peiling peeked into the oven. It was empty.

"Oh, I'm steaming it," said Mama, pointing to a huge covered pot on the stove. "It's not so dry that way . . ."

The doorbell rang. They heard Baba stumping through the hallway to open the door. It was Great-Aunt Shuhua, Baba's aunt. Usually she let herself in through the side door, but in honor of the occasion she had come to the front door and rung the bell. Baba followed her into the kitchen, carrying an enormous bowl of salad.

"I hope I made enough," Great-Aunt Shuhua said in Taiwanese. "I put in six heads of lettuce . . ."

Mama peered into the bowl. A volcano of greenery threatened to erupt over the rim.

"It should be plenty," Mama said.

Then Auntie Huiyan and Uncle Paul arrived. Uncle Paul lugged a huge casserole dish of candied yams, while Auntie Huiyan, who was young and pretty, tripped in with an armful of gaily wrapped presents. One after another the other aunties and uncles began to arrive, also by the front door, each bearing a new "American" dish they had concocted. There were fruitcake, baked ham, and mashed potatoes.

In the kitchen, Mama let everyone peep at the steaming turkey. Then Mama uncovered a huge platter on the counter, revealing a golden-brown mountain of what looked like fried meat cutlets.

"What's that?" Uncle Samson asked, slipping in the side door. He wore a black turtleneck sweater, and a small diamond stud flashed in his ear. He was carrying a large plastic tub filled with eggnog. Printed in faded letters on the side of the tub was the legend, "Super Bowl XXXVIII."

"It's chicken-fried steak. It's a traditional American dish," Mama said proudly. "I got the recipe from a magazine Peiling gave me."

Uncle Samson wrinkled his brow. "Is it chicken, or is it steak? How can it be both?"

"It's steak," Mama explained. "But it's steak that you treat like it's chicken. You coat it and deep-fry it like you're making fried chicken. That's why it's called 'chicken-fried.'"

"Oh, I see," everyone said.

Just then, the doorbell rang yet again. Mystified, Peiling ran to answer it. Who could it be? She thought that everyone had already arrived. She flung the front door open. Miss Rosenweig was standing there, locking her bicycle to the porch railing. She had traded her Birkenstocks for a pair of high-heeled boots, and sparkling stones dangled from her ears, but she wore the same fluorescent lime green bike helmet. She took a bottle of Manischewitz out of one of her panniers.

"What are you doing here?" Peiling gasped.

"Hello, Peiling. Your mother invited me. Didn't she tell you?" Miss Rosenweig replied, ducking to avoid being hit by the inflatable Santa as it bobbed in the stiff wind. "I've come to celebrate Christmas with you."

Standing with her hand on the doorknob, Peiling felt a sudden wave of awkwardness. She felt as if Miss Rosenweig had just walked in on her playing dress-up with someone else's clothes.

"But I thought you didn't celebrate Christmas," Peiling blurted out.

Miss Rosenweig smiled. "I thought you didn't either."

Peiling managed to take Miss Rosenweig's coat and lead her to the living room, where the aunties and uncles were sipping Uncle Samson's eggnog. Then she dashed back into the kitchen with the wine.

"Why is Miss Rosenweig here?" she hissed at Mama.

"Didn't you say she was Jewish? So her family doesn't celebrate Christmas either. I thought she might be lonely all by herself with nothing to do."

"Couldn't she just go see a movie?" Peiling muttered.

Mama ignored her. She was jabbing impatiently at a potato with a pair of chopsticks. "Who knew these things took so long to cook?" she said, wiping her brow. "They're done, finally. Go tell everyone that dinner's ready."

Baba came into the kitchen. He caught sight of the enormous turkey steaming on the cutting board. He took out a cleaver and was about to whack it into bite-size pieces.

Mama waved her hands at him. "No, no! Carve it at the dining room table," she cried. "American-style, re-member!"

Baba carried out the turkey on a large platter as Mama took off her apron and fluffed her hair. She and Peiling brought the last of the side dishes to the dining room table. Uncle Samson had lit the candles, and was pouring a finger or two of wine into each glass. Baba stood carving the turkey into neat slices. He had put on a fresh shirt and tie, and looked surprisingly handsome and dignified. Everyone drew around the table and took their seats, the candlelight shining on their faces and gleaming on the glasses and silverware.

Baba cut the last slice and made room for the platter on the lazy Susan. Then he turned the lazy Susan so the turkey stopped in front of Miss Rosenweig.

"*Jabeng.*" He waved his arms at the food. " 'Eat, eat.' That's what we say in Taiwan. Merry Christmas," he added as an afterthought.

Miss Rosenweig raised her glass to him, smiling. "*L'chaim.* That's what we say at my house. It means 'To life.' " She served herself a slice of turkey breast.

Soon the lazy Susan was turning nonstop as everyone helped themselves to turkey and the side dishes. It was so heavy with food that it creaked.

Peiling waited until the grown-ups had served themselves. Then she turned the lazy Susan so the turkey was in front of her. She used the serving fork to take a piece of leg meat and a slice of breast. She heaped her plate with stuffing. There was a little bit of empty space left at the edge of the plate. She took a scoop of the salad that Great-Aunt Shuhua had made.

Sighing with anticipation, she forked some turkey. But as she brought it toward her mouth, she noticed that the skin, instead of being crisp and golden, was brown and rubbery, with flecks of some green leaf. She took a bite. It squelched mushily between her teeth. She grabbed a napkin to stop herself from spitting it out.

"I marinated it with ginger and soy sauce to make it more tender . . ." Mama's proud voice floated over the dinner table.

Peiling took a bite of the stuffing to get the taste of turkey out of her mouth. This time she could barely pry her teeth apart. Instead of bread crumbs, it had been made of sticky rice, studded with shiitake mushrooms and dried shrimp.

Surely the salad would be safe. Hastily, she took a bite. Hidden beneath a lettuce leaf, something round and soft squirted sweet juice into her mouth. This time, she couldn't stop herself from spitting it out. It lay white and limp in her napkin. It was a kind of fruit called *longyan*, or "dragon's eye." She crumpled it up in her napkin, and then looked around furtively to see whether anyone else noticed how awful the food was.

Baba was helping himself to another piece of chicken-fried steak. "Hmmm, American food's not so bad," he was saying.

"Wonderful!" Miss Rosenweig exclaimed, eating the salad. "What's in the dressing?"

"Sesame oil," said Great-Aunt Shuhua importantly, looking triumphantly at the other aunts. "Also, I put in *longyan* for sweetness, and water chestnuts for crunch."

Peiling kept her eyes on her plate, writhing with embarrassment. She was sure that Miss Rosenweig was just being polite.

At last, dinner was over. Peiling led everyone to the piano so they could sing carols. She opened the book of carols to the "Twelve Days of Christmas" and struck the opening chords. Gamely the aunties and uncles struggled through a few choruses.

"Calling birds, partridges," grumbled Great-Aunt Shuhua, breaking off in the middle of a verse. "Who can keep them straight?"

"Hmmm," said Peiling, hastily flipping through the pages of the carol book. "How about 'Jingle Bells'?"

But it was too late. Bored, Uncle Wenbao was already taking the karaoke machine out of the cupboard and hooking it up to the TV. Before Peiling could protest, he was crooning the theme song from his favorite Chinese soap opera. Uncle Paul and Auntie Huiyan grabbed the twin mics and teamed up for a Taiwanese love duet.

Miss Rosenweig sat on the couch, clapping along with the beat. Uncle Samson sat down next to her.

"Probably not how you celebrate Hanukkah, huh?" Peiling heard him say.

Miss Rosenweig laughed and shook her head. "My family would never do this."

"Why not?"

"Too uptight."

"What would they do instead?" Uncle Samson asked.

"Play games, probably."

"We play games too," Uncle Samson said. "Mahjong, mostly, but sometimes bridge."

"Mahjong?" Great-Aunt Shuhua cried, pricking up her ears. "Did anyone say mahjong?"

Peiling shook her head frantically from the piano bench. Uncle Samson saw her. "Not tonight, Auntie," he said. "Maybe another time."

But Great-Aunt Shuhua either ignored or didn't hear him. She was already rummaging in the cabinet for the mahjong tiles. They were kept in an old box of embroidered yellow brocade. Great-Aunt Shuhua carried the box to the card table and dumped the tiles out.

Miss Rosenweig went over. She fingered the yellow brocade. "This is beautiful," she said. Then she picked up a tile. "How pretty. Could someone teach me how to play?"

"Of course," said Baba, drawing an extra chair over to the card table. "I'll explain the rules to you, and we'll play a hand together."

"Wenbao! Samdala!" Great-Aunt Shuhua barked imperiously. She called Uncle Paul by his Taiwanese name, Samdala. Obediently the two uncles went over to the table and began to help her stack the tiles.

Peiling turned to the piano, trying to fight the tears that she felt rising. She started to bang out "Jingle Bells" as loudly as she could.

"Cool it, Peiling." It was Uncle Samson. "Come on. I need your help to build a fire."

She shook her head, stubbornly pounding out the chords.

"Look, I have a surprise for you." Uncle Samson drew a small paper packet out of his pocket. Curious, Peiling stopped playing. He opened it to reveal a handful of round brown objects that looked a little like acorns.

She stared at them, mystified. "What are they?" she asked.

"Chestnuts," Uncle Samson said. "You know, as in chestnuts roasting on an open you-know-what. Help me make one, okay? Go on. Go get the matches."

She ran to get them. When she came back, he was kneeling on the hearth crumpling old newspaper and arranging sticks of dry wood. Then he struck a match and lit the fire, fanning the orange flames with a sheet of folded newspaper.

"Where do you suppose we put the chestnuts?" he said.

"I don't know."

Shrugging, Uncle Samson took them out of the bag and used the poker to line them up in a row a few inches in front of the fire. "We'll see if this works."

"Ai-ya!" There was a shrill exclamation from the card table. Great-Aunt Shuhua was staring at Miss Rosenweig's hand. "You got a 'long dragon'! Not bad for a beginner!" she cried. Great-Aunt Shuhua looked at Miss Rosenweig with new respect.

Then she added in Taiwanese to Baba, "Such a pretty girl. Not married, you say? What a shame!"

Mama, who had been in the kitchen, came into the living room with her best teapot and a plate of cookies. She took one look at the mahjong table. In an under-voice she said to Uncle Samson sharply, "Why didn't you stop Auntie?"

"I tried to, but I couldn't," he muttered back.

Mama said loudly, "Come on, everyone! Let's have some tea and the cookies that Peiling made." She carried the tea over to the coffee table next to the Christmas tree. "Time to open presents!"

Baba and Miss Rosenweig and the uncles rose from the mahjong table.

"Just one more game," Great-Aunt Shuhua said.

"No, no," Mama said firmly. She steered Great-Aunt Shuhua by the elbow over to the Christmas tree. "Look, I made your favorite tea, Dragon Well. Drink it while it's hot."

While Mama passed around the cookies and poured out the tea, everyone gathered around the tree.

"Here, Peiling. This is for you." Miss Rosenweig gave Peiling a small, flat package.

"For me?" Peiling said, tearing open the wrapping. Inside was the most beautiful book she had ever seen. It had real ferns and flower petals embedded in its cover of textured paper. She opened it eagerly. It was blank.

"It's a journal, Peiling, for you to record things that are important to you, that you want to remember," Miss Rosenweig explained.

"Oh," Peiling said, flatly. She couldn't imagine that she would ever have anything important enough to write in such a book.

Mama stooped to pick up a brightly wrapped package from the pile under the tree. "This is for you, Miss Rosenweig."

"Oh, you really didn't have to," Miss Rosenweig said smilingly, opening the present. It was a book on the Chinese zodiac. On the cover was a chart with the twelve animals arranged in a wheel, telling you what animal you were if you were born in a given year. Underneath, the title blared, *The Chinese Zodiac: Unleashing Your Potential and Finding the Perfect Mate.*

"This looks fascinating," Miss Rosenweig said. "Thank you very much."

Uncle Samson glanced at the book. "I can't believe you got her this," he said to Mama. "You don't believe in that stuff, do you?"

"Why not? Let's see here. You're a boar, and it says that boars are headstrong and impolite. Also that boars don't get along with snakes," Mama retorted. "Your last girlfriend was a snake."

"And that's proof?"

Mama nodded pityingly, and smiled apologetically at Miss Rosenweig. "Some people find it so hard to accept the truth about themselves." She turned back to Uncle Samson. "Fang Lili is an ox, by the way," she added casually.

Peiling wasn't sure who was more embarrassed—she or Uncle Samson. Uncle Samson went over to the stereo and began to fiddle with the knobs and dials, even though the music was perfectly clear. Peiling ran into the kitchen to refill the plate of cookies. In the dark, empty kitchen she leaned her cheeks against the frosty window to cool her burning face.

She caught a glimpse of her own reflection in the black window. Her black hair was sweaty and clung in damp clumps to her cheeks and forehead. She had a big grease spot on the front of her dress. Her tights bunched around her ankles, like an elephant's skin. Reflected behind her, the usually spotless kitchen looked like a disaster area, with its platters of half-eaten food and towers of dirty dishes. She jerked her head away from her reflection and ran back to the living room.

Baba was just unwrapping the plaque of Taiwan. He chuckled in a pleased way when he saw it. "How'd you make this?"

Peiling couldn't answer. She just shook her head dumbly.

"This is for you, Peiling," Uncle Samson pressed a red envelope into her hand. She opened it. It was a pair of tickets to the Ice Capades.

Uncle Samson bent down to whisper in her ear. "It's at the beginning of February," he said. "We'll go and have a hot fudge sundae afterwards."

Ordinarily, she would have been thrilled, but tonight all she could manage was a stifled thank you. He gave her hand a squeeze, as if he realized how Christmas had disappointed her.

She dragged herself through the rest of the evening. At long last everyone said good-bye and went home. Wearily, Peiling helped Mama and Baba clean up before going to bed. When she went to the living room to collect the dirty teacups and crumb-covered plates, she suddenly remembered the chestnuts that Uncle Samson had brought. She had forgotten all about them. She stooped down before the fire, now just smoldering logs in a pile of ash. The chestnuts had all been burnt black.

13

On the first day of school after Christmas vacation, Peiling returned to school relieved that she had something to say when the kids asked each other about their presents.

When she walked into Drama Club, the first person she saw was Simon Pence.

"Hey, Peiling, what'd you get for Christmas?" he said.

"Clothes, tickets, books," she said mechanically. She was about to turn away before Simon could start boasting about his own presents, when she noticed that his right arm was in a cast.

"What happened?" she asked, pointing.

"Broke it snowboarding," Simon said nonchalantly. "That's what I got for Christmas, a snowboard."

Peiling hesitated before saying, "Will you be able to be in the play?"

"Sure. No worries," Simon said. "I'll get the cast off in a couple of weeks. But the cool thing is that I'll get out of homework in the meantime."

"Shhhh!" Mrs. Baldino hissed. "We're running through Act Three now!"

Laura was already onstage, tapping her foot impatiently. Peiling hurried backstage. She almost tripped over Madeline, wearing her costume and sitting cross-legged cuddling some sort of stuffed animal in her lap.

"Look what I got for Christmas," Madeline whispered. "It's a Furbie. See? It talks and eats and everything . . ."

"Come on, Madeline. Why don't I do something about your sleeves?" Peiling said wearily. She got a needle and thread from the prop room and began to take in the extra fabric on Madeline's sleeves.

From offstage she could see and hear Laura speaking her lines. The prince had already exchanged clothes with the pauper and been thrown out of the palace. Now, wearing the pauper's tatters, Laura was making her way through London, trying in vain to prove that she was the prince.

"Touch not my sacred person with thy filthy hands!" Laura declaimed to an incredulous rabble. "I tell you, I am Edward, Prince of Wales!"

As usual, Laura knew her lines perfectly. She recited them so clearly that each word rung like a bell through the whole auditorium. All of the gestures that Mrs. Baldino had coached her in—the toss of her royal head, the stamp of her royal foot—she had down pat. It could have been the performance itself, rather than a rehearsal weeks before.

An innkeeper, weary of this ragged boy claiming to be the prince, cuffed him and sent him sprawling to the ground. "Be off, thou crazy rubbish!"

Laura raised herself from the ground. She put her shaking hand to her bleeding lip. Peiling knew that the "blood" was red paint dabbed from a sponge that Laura had secreted in her hand. "As forlorn and friendless as I be, I tell ye again, you unmannerly cur, I am the Prince of Wales!"

Peiling turned her eyes away. She felt hard-hearted, indifferent. What was so great about being in the play, anyway? She watched Laura, who was supposed to be such a great actress. Yet Peiling felt nothing, not the slightest pity, for the prince's plight. They were just empty words, posturing. At least with props you had something solid to show for your work. Deliberately she stabbed her needle through the layers of Madeline's costume.

"Ouch, Peiling," Madeline complained, rubbing her arm. "You almost pricked me."

In the classroom, Steven tore open a two-pack of double-A batteries and was putting them into the new digital camera he had gotten for Christmas. One of them dropped on the floor. It rolled and hit Grace in the foot. Grace, who was in the middle of showing

Peiling her new drawing pencils, picked it up and was about to toss it to him, when suddenly her eyes opened wide and she stared fixedly at the shiny silver cylinder in her hand.

"I was thinking the other day that if we made the chicken out of something metallic, something shiny, it would really stand out. *Why not batteries?* They come in different shapes and sizes, and probably everybody has a bunch of used ones lying around at home somewhere . . ."

"I know I must have, like, fifty of 'em," Steven nodded.

Grace bounded to her feet. "Found objects!" she exclaimed. "Making art out of what other people throw away . . ."

"How was everyone's vacation?" Miss Rosenweig cried, bursting into the room with a big cardboard box. Underneath her bike helmet, her face was glowing with excitement. "Boy, did I get a great idea for our Winter Project!"

Without even taking off her helmet, Miss Rosenweig dumped the box out on her desk. Out tumbled bolts of different materials, red and green and orange and blue.

She unrolled a red cloth embroidered with golden dragons. "Does anyone know what this is?"

No one did.

"It's silk brocade. It's from China." She unrolled a cloth patterned with red, green, and black zigzags. "And this is *kente* from Africa. And this is a Black Watch plaid from Scotland, and this is a paisley from India . . .

"Here's my idea," she cried. "For the background, we'll cut out all the countries from the different materials and make a map of the world."

"And in the foreground," Grace jumped in. "We'll make the chicken out of batteries!" She explained her idea.

Miss Rosenweig bobbed her head, her eyes sparkling. She was so pleased that she hugged Grace. "What a super idea!" She glanced nervously at the calendar. "But we'd better get to work. There're only three more weeks left to go."

Peiling looked up dully. She seemed to watch their happiness and excitement as if from a great distance. Well, whatever tasks they gave her, she would do. Maybe it would even help her keep her mind off her troubles. And she was grateful for one thing. At least she didn't have to write an essay on "What I Did Over Christmas Vacation."

After lunch, Laura Hamilton, instead of cutting out Indonesia from a piece of batik, was going on and on about the cell phone she had gotten for Christmas, and how surprised she was when she opened the package. "The very first thing I did was flip it open and call up my grandfather to thank him!"

Laura glanced over at Peiling and called out, "Hey, Peiling. How was your Christmas? Did you retile the bathroom again?" She said it good-naturedly, and laughed in a friendly way.

Miss Rosenweig, walking by with a pair of pinking shears, said, "I went to Peiling's for Christmas. It was absolutely wonderful." She gave Peiling a big smile. "In fact, that was where I came up with my idea. I saw their silk brocade mahjong box . . ."

Laura's jaw dropped with surprise. Peiling could tell from Laura's expression that she was jealous that Miss Rosenweig had spent Christmas at the Wangs. Laura waited until Miss Rosenweig was out of earshot before saying waspishly, "What'd you have, chicken chow mein?"

Suddenly, Peiling was shaking with anger. "Shut up!" she shouted. "You make me sick, Laura Hamilton!" She threw down her scissors and walked away, but not before she had seen the hurt and surprised look on Laura's face.

She sat by herself in a corner.

"Are you okay?" Grace came over to sit beside her.

Peiling shook her head.

"What's wrong?" said Grace.

"Everything," said Peiling. Grace had spent her Christmas vacation with her grandparents in Florida, and had only gotten back the day before. After a pause Peiling corrected herself, "No. Not everything. Just Christmas."

"But Miss Rosenwieg just said she had a wonderful time," Grace protested.

"No, it was a total disaster." Peiling found herself pouring out the story of her Christmas. How excited she had been, how the preparations seemed to be going so beautifully, but then the letdown: how dreadful the food had been, how the carols had been replaced by karaoke, how Great-Aunt Shuhua had insisted on playing mahjong.

Grace giggled. "Miss Rosenweig beat your great-aunt at mahjong? I'd like to have seen that."

"But it wasn't funny. It was all wrong!"

"Why?" asked Grace.

"Because you don't play mahjong at Christmas!"

"What does it matter, as long as it's fun?"

"You don't understand," Peiling said. "I just wanted to have a simple Christmas like everyone else—"

"Like everyone else?" Grace stared at her in disbelief. "Why would you want to be like everyone else?"

Peiling looked back at her friend despairingly. How could she explain to Grace, whose tastes and interests were totally different from everyone else's, but who never seemed the least bothered by it? She thought back to how she had first met Grace. The first week of kindergarten, Peiling had been sent to talk to the principal for crying too much in school. Grace had been sitting outside the office waiting to see the principal too. Her crime was "destroying school property." She had clogged the girls' bathroom toilet by trying to flush a Barbie doll.

Grace seemed to realize that she wasn't helping. She moved closer to Peiling and said, "Why don't you talk to your uncle?"

Peiling shook her head miserably. "He hasn't been coming to the house. Mama wants to set him up with some girl from work, and he doesn't want her to, so he hasn't been coming by."

"Grace," Miss Rosenweig called from the other end of the room, holding up two pieces of cloth. "What do you think would be better for the ocean? Black velvet or blue?"

"Let me take a look." Grace hurried away.

Peiling hugged her knees to her chest and put her face down on them. Her head was filled with thoughts she couldn't even put into words: how Mama had stood up for her, about Baba and the fried oyster pancakes, about *Zhongguo* and *Meiguo*. She remembered the tiny band of Taiwanese athletes marching under their unfamiliar flag when she watched the Olympics, and the time she had gone to the bank months ago, when the teller had made Baba repeat everything because she claimed not to understand his accent. She remembered last New Year's when Uncle Samson's then-girlfriend Cindy had grimaced and buried her fluffy blonde head in Uncle Samson's coat every time a firecracker went off.

She wasn't like Grace, Peiling realized. A part of her

wanted to be like everyone else. Or if she were to be different, she wanted to choose it, not to have her difference forced on her. She had wanted to celebrate Christmas to make her feel more like everyone else. But then everything that had happened made her feel more different, more alone, different and alone even from her own family. Oh, she knew that Mama and Uncle Samson and even Baba had tried their hardest to give her a good Christmas, but somehow that made it even worse. Even with their best efforts, she couldn't seem to get what other people had without even trying.

She had held in her mind a perfect Christmas, like the Hamiltons' golden carousel, lovelier and more dazzling from every angle. Now the image was so blurred and smudged that she couldn't ever believe in it. She would never try to celebrate Christmas again.

The bell rang. School was finally over. As Peiling plodded out to the school bus she heard someone behind her call, "Peiling, could I talk to you for a moment?"

She turned around. It was Miss Rosenweig. She ran a few steps to catch up with Peiling, the wooden heels of her clogs clicking on the ground, her ponytail bobbing as she ran.

"Please thank your mother again for inviting me to Christmas at your house," Miss Rosenweig said. "I really enjoyed myself."

Peiling nodded. She looked away. She was afraid that

the next thing Miss Rosenweig said would be about how wonderfully multicultural the Wang Christmas had been. Peiling knew Miss Rosenweig meant well, but somehow she couldn't bear to hear it. She thought she might gag, or cry.

Instead, Miss Rosenweig said casually, "I tried to cook that chicken-fried steak that your mother made for Christmas, but it was nowhere as good as hers. Could you get the recipe for me?"

Peiling stared at her. "Mama's chicken-fried steak?" She shook her head dully. "It wasn't her own recipe. She just got it from a magazine."

Miss Rosenweig smiled. "I'm afraid the recipe from the magazine wouldn't do me any good." She fell into step beside Peiling and walked with her along the row of waiting buses. "A really good cook never just follows a recipe, Peiling. She always adds some secret ingredient or special touch to make it her own. That's why her food is so much more delicious than everyone else's." She put her hand on Peiling's shoulder, and looked down at Peiling's disbelieving face, laughing. "Ask your mother about the recipe. You'll see."

Mama's car was already in the driveway when Peiling got home. She used her key to let herself into the garage. She went into the kitchen and replaced her shoes with slippers.

She crept into the family room. Mama was sitting on the sofa resting after work, reading the newspaper with her slippered feet stretched out on the coffee table before her and her reading glasses perched on her nose. In one hand she held a pencil with which she underlined words she didn't understand. Beside her was a worn English–Chinese pocket dictionary.

Peiling knelt on the floor in front of her. "Mama, when you made the chicken-fried steak for Christmas, did you follow the recipe in the magazine?"

Mama took off her glasses, surprised. "Yes," she said hesitantly.

"Did you do exactly what it said? Did you change anything?" Peiling persisted. She wasn't even sure now what she wanted Mama to say, *Yes, I changed it* or *No, I followed every word*.

Mama looked wary, and then defensive, an expression which Peiling had almost never seen on her face, as if she had been caught in some wrongdoing. She put down the newspaper and sat up straight and tall on the sofa. "All right," she said, her jaw tight. "I added a pinch of five-spice powder to the coating. Otherwise," she added defiantly, "it would have been totally bland."

Peiling looked up at Mama's flushed face. So Miss Rosenweig had been right after all. A secret ingredient. A special touch. Baba always said that it only took one bite for him to recognize a dish that Mama made, whether it was the "two friends of winter" or eight-treasure rice.

"The truth is, I always change recipes," Mama continued, her voice hard and a little bitter. "But maybe I won't do it anymore, since you don't seem to like it."

"I—I . . ." Peiling didn't know what to say.

Mama said abruptly, "Do you know why we came to the States, Peiling?"

Peiling was surprised. She shook her head. Mama and Baba had never talked about why they had immigrated before.

Mama fidgeted with the dictionary. "Baba didn't want to come. Both of our families were in Taiwan. But I thought things in Taiwan were too small, like this . . ." She put her hands close together like two walls closing in on each other.

" 'Feeding ducks.' That's what they called how the children were taught at schools, like cramming stuff down their throats. All this memorization, and no chance for creativity. Just like following recipes word for word, with never any chance to—what's the word?—improvise. That's how it was when I was a kid, and I didn't want that for you.

"So we came here, so you could get a different kind of education. A teacher like Miss Rosenweig—" Mama's hands sketched big circles in the air around her head to suggest the wild disarray of Miss Rosenweig's hair. "She would never have been hired in Taiwan . . ."

Mama sighed. She was still playing with the dictionary. A loose page fluttered out. Absently she slid it back into the wrong place. "It was a big adjustment. Baba and I were already over thirty. We were always surprised at how different things were. I remember the first time your school had a bake sale, to raise money for a new playground.

"I made *danta*, a kind of custard pie with a very difficult crust, very crumbly, very difficult to shape. But no one bought a single one. They just sat there on the table, untouched, like the Americans thought they were poison or something. After that, I bought an American cookbook and learned to make chocolate chip cookies." Mama laughed a little, but her mouth had a bitter twist to it. Suddenly Peiling saw how proud and sensitive Mama was under her brisk, practical outside.

"After we got here, then all my brothers and sisters wanted to come. Even Baba's Aunt Shuhua. I sponsored them all and helped them apply for visas. When they got here, whenever they had questions about the United States—how to open a bank account, how to buy insurance—they would always call and ask me, because I had gotten here first." She laughed again, looking down at the dictionary in her lap. "But I guess I'm not as much of an expert as they thought."

There was a silence. Mama stared at her feet. Then she shut the dictionary with a snap and swung her feet onto the floor. She stood up. "Why is everyone so interested in my chicken-fried steak all of a sudden?" she cried. Suddenly, Peiling saw that her mouth was working and puckering like she was about to cry.

Peiling scooted forward. She put her arms around her mother's knees and held them tight. "It was so delicious, that's why. Miss Rosenweig stopped me at school today to find out how you made it. That's why I asked."

"Really?" Mama said, a little suspicious.

"Yes, really," Peiling said, looking up at her. "Could you write out the recipe for her?"

"Did she really like it so much?" Mama asked skeptically. She patted Peiling's head, and gently detached herself from Peiling's grasp. She stepped over to the shelf next to the TV. She blew her nose in a tissue. But then she pulled out the magazine that Peiling had given her. She sat down at the little desk where she made phone calls and paid bills. She smoothed out the magazine. Then she got out a pen and began to copy the recipe onto a sheet of notebook paper.

While Mama was writing, Peiling went to the kitchen. She opened up the spice cabinet. There it was on the second shelf, a small bottle labeled "five-spice powder" with a bunch of Chinese characters underneath. She didn't recognize any of them except for *wu*, the character for five. She stuck her finger in the bottle and licked off the dusty brown grains. It was bitter and biting on her tongue. Its spicy heat seemed to shoot up into her sinuses, making her nose tingle; but then the woody perfume of cinnamon filled her mouth, and she tasted the lingering, sweetish flavor of licorice at the back of her throat. She put the bottle back on the shelf.

When she went back to the living room, Mama handed the recipe to her. "By the way," she said casually. "Why don't you invite your teacher for Chinese New Year? She clearly appreciates good Chinese cooking."

"Chicken–fried steak?" Peiling asked doubtfully. "Maybe I will," she said slowly.

14

"So do they fit?" Mama asked.

Peiling pulled on the new pair of dark blue corduroys that Mama had bought her for Chinese New Year. She turned and looked at herself in the mirror. The waist and hips were neither too loose nor too tight, and the cuffs hit just above her heel.

Mama stood back to look at Peiling. "Should I take the hem up half an inch?" she wondered. "No, they'll be just right when you have your shoes on. I worried that they might be too long, but you're growing so fast, soon you'll be able to fit my clothes." Mama laughed, but when she put her hand on Peiling's head as if to see how tall she was, she looked a little sad.

Baba stuck his head in. "We'd better leave soon. I told the aunties and uncles to meet us at the restaurant at noon."

Mama glanced at her watch. "We can't go yet. I told Fang Lili to meet us here."

Baba blinked. "What? You asked her to come here? What will Samson say?" he added in an undervoice.

Mama shrugged, doing her best to look nonchalant.

From her bedroom window, Peiling saw a lipstick-red VW Beetle pull up to the house. A young woman with shoulder-length black hair and a red wool coat came briskly up the front walk carrying a huge shopping bag. The doorbell rang. Mama ran downstairs to open the door.

"Happy New Year, Auntie!" Peiling heard a bright voice chirp in Chinese. "Thanks so much for inviting me."

"Peiling! Wenzhe!" Mama's voice floated upstairs. "Come down and meet Miss Fang."

Peiling followed Baba down the stairs. Fang Lili was standing in the hallway with a big smile. She wore pink lipstick and pearl earrings. When she saw Baba she put her hands together and made a little bow. She said "*Bofu,*" which means "Uncle." When she saw Peiling, she ran forward and gave her a little hug. "I've heard so much about you," she said, switching to English. "Your mother told me you liked Nintendo, so I brought you some games."

She opened the shopping bag to reveal a towering stack of new video games.

"Thank you," Peiling said, a little stunned.

Behind Mama and Fang Lili's backs, Baba and Peiling looked at each other. Baba looked up at the ceiling and shook his head slightly. Peiling knew what he meant. Fang Lili didn't seem like Uncle Samson's type at all.

In the car on the way to the restaurant, Fang Lili sat in back with Peiling. She kept asking Peiling questions about her school, what subjects Peiling liked, and what she liked to play with. "The Xbox, what do you think of the Xbox?" Peiling wondered if Fang Lili would get one for her if she said she liked it.

When Peiling could get a word in edgewise, she said, "Shouldn't we have made that turn? Li Hua's on Payne Street, isn't it?"

"Oh, didn't we tell you? We're not going to Li Hua," Baba said from the driver's seat. "Mama saw an ad for a new Chinese restaurant in the newspaper. We've decided to give that a try."

Peiling was surprised. "But we always go to Li Hua," she said.

"Well, maybe it's time for a change," Baba said.

They pulled up in front of an imposing-looking building with a sign reading, "Ocean Jewels Seafood Restaurant." Above the sign was a red banner proclaiming, "GRAND OPENING."

When they went in, Peiling saw that it was a lot fancier than Li Hua. Instead of red vinyl banquettes, there were snow-white tablecloths and upholstered wooden chairs. On the walls were Chinese landscape paintings in black ink, instead of garish calendars with photos of Hong Kong movie stars and pop singers, like at the old place. All the tables were crowded with Chinese families eating and drinking. Peiling always wondered where all those Chinese families came from. When she was at school or the mall or the library, she never saw anyone

Chinese. But come Chinese New Year, suddenly dozens of black-haired, chopstick-wielding families seemed to materialize out of nowhere.

The aunties and uncles were already seated at a big round table in the corner.

"Where's Samson?" Mama said, hurrying over to them.

"Peiling's teacher called to say her bicycle had a flat tire," Great-Aunt Shuhua said. "Samson went to get her. They should be here any moment."

"Did you order yet?" Mama said. She herded Baba and Peiling to the empty seats on the far side of the table. However, she waved Fang Lili towards the row of three empty seats next to Great-Aunt Shuhua, so that Uncle Samson, Peiling realized, would be forced to sit near her when he came.

"Yes, we ordered," Uncle Paul said. "They said they'd start serving as soon as everyone got here."

At that moment, Uncle Samson and Miss Rosenweig appeared. Mama rose, beaming. "Lili, I want to introduce you to my younger brother Samson, and to Peiling's teacher, Miss Rosenweig."

"Call me Deanna," Miss Rosenweig said, sitting down on one side of Fang Lili. Uncle Samson took the seat on Fang Lili's other side.

The waiter, in white jacket and black pants, placed *guotie*, pan-fried dumplings, and fried noodles on the lazy Susan. Peiling, who was starving, took a big helping of each. But when she bit into her first dumpling, her teeth could barely meet through the thick, doughy skin. The filling was unpleasantly salty. She tried the noodles. They were so greasy that they slipped off her chopsticks. She chewed thoughtfully. Even though the décor was so much sleeker here, the food really wasn't very tasty. She found herself wishing that they had just gone to Li Hua.

Across the table, Fang Lili was asking Uncle Samson about his job. Even though her English was excellent, she would occasionally slip in a Chinese or Taiwanese word.

"What did you say?" Uncle Samson would say, wrinkling his brow. "Oh! You mean, '*cost of living increase,*'" he would say, translating the word into English. Then he would turn to Miss Rosenweig and address some comment to her.

"So you teach elementary school?" Fang Lili said, turning to Miss Rosenweig also. "I really admire you. You must be very brave. They say that even elementary school students can be quite unruly here in the United States."

"Oh, I wouldn't say so. I love it," Miss Rosenweig said. "In fact, I think I learn as much from them as they learn from me," she added, giving Peiling a smile.

Just as a big steamer of *nian gao*, sticky rice cake, was being served for dessert, Uncle Paul cleared his throat impressively. "Huiyan and I have an important announcement to make." Peiling looked at him curiously. Usually Uncle Paul talked about golf and the stock market, but today his face was pink with pride and excitement. "We just went to the doctor's yesterday," he burst out. "Huiyan is going to have a baby in July!"

Everyone at the table erupted into smiles and congratulations.

"Do you know if it's going to be a boy or a girl?" Peiling asked eagerly. It would be her first cousin born in the United States.

"It's going to be a girl," Auntie Huiyan said happily.

"Have you thought about a name?" Mama asked.

"What do you think of the name Wang Suwen?" Uncle Paul asked her. "Isn't that a nice name?"

"But what about Susan Wang?" Auntie Huiyan interrupted him. "Isn't that a nice name, too?"

A voice crackled over the loudspeaker, in English first, and then Chinese. "Honored guests, the lion dance is about to begin in the parking lot."

The restaurant emptied out as everyone put on their coats and went outside. In the parking lot, the great fringed red-and-gold lion's head, supported by the lead dancer, bobbed and swayed, as the body and tail, made up of four dancers draped in silver and red cloth, lashed back and forth. Strings of firecrackers went off with bangs and flashes between their prancing feet, as the gongs clanged faster and faster.

Was it Peiling's imagination, or were the lion dancers not as good as at Li Hua either? It seemed to her that there was no heart to their performance. Their leaps weren't explosive enough, their kicks not as high. Even the firecrackers didn't sound as loud.

Peiling sighed, huddling into her down coat. She could remember celebrating Chinese New Year every year since they had come to Ohio. She remembered when she had been so small that she had to sit on Baba's shoulders in order to see the lion dancers over the heads of everyone else. She remembered how Uncle Samson, who had been in college in Pennsylvania then, had driven all night to join them, since he didn't get Chinese New Year off from his school.

Year after year, they had gone through the same old round for Chinese New Year, cleaning the house, buying new clothes, visiting relatives, and then the Chinese restaurant with the lion dancers. It had become a tired routine, like brushing her teeth before going to bed. She didn't prepare for it or look forward to it. Not like for Christmas, when all her preparations seemed fraught with hope and meaning, almost as exciting as the day itself. No, instead Chinese New Year crept up behind her. She forgot all about it until it was upon her again, and Mama was lugging out the vacuum cleaner, and cutting up old undershirts for rags. She had always taken it for granted. But this year she could catch the whiff of change in the air. And now that Chinese New Year was in danger of changing, she realized how much she wanted it to stay the same.

The last strings of firecrackers lay smoldering and smoking on the ground. The lion dance was over. Baba went inside to pay the check. Fang Lili had gotten something on her contact lens, and had to run to the bathroom. Uncle Paul and Auntie Huiyan, who turned out to live not far from Miss Rosenweig, offered to give her a ride home. Uncle Samson waved and headed toward his green Mitsubishi.

"Wait!" Mama called. "I haven't given you your New Year's present yet."

She pulled a red envelope out of her pocketbook.

Uncle Samson came back. His anger, which he had tried to hide all through lunch, was now plain on his face. "Shuli, you invited Fang Lili even though I told you I didn't want to meet her."

Mama tried to act casual. "So, what's the big deal? She's a friend of mine, and so what if I ask her to join us . . ."

"Don't give me that," Uncle Samson said sharply. "It's obvious that you're trying to set me up. And it's also obvious that you think that just because she's Taiwanese, that she and I have a lot in common."

He shook his head disgustedly. "When are you going to learn that I'm grown up, Shuli? Old enough to make my own decisions. And when are you going to learn that they might not be the same as yours?"

The red envelope was still in Mama's hand. He plucked it from her fingers and put it back in her pocket book. "I'm twenty-six now. I don't need this."

"But elders are supposed to give their youngers New

Year's money," Mama protested, trying to make him take it.

"Not in America. And besides," he added. "I make almost as much as you and Wenzhe put together."

Mama shut her mouth, looking as if she had been slapped in the face.

Uncle Samson unlocked his car and was about to get in. Suddenly he came back. "I almost forgot." He handed Peiling a brown paper bag. "I brought these, like you asked me to." Without waiting for her to reply, he got into his car and drove off. She opened the bag. It was filled with batteries.

15

It was January twenty-fourth, the last day before the Winter Assembly. Peiling, Grace, Sandra, and Miss Rosenweig had stayed after school to finish the collage. All the countries had been glued onto the velvet-covered plywood. Miss Rosenweig was using an iron to carefully press them flat. Peiling and Sandra were busy sorting the last-minute influx of extra batteries the class had brought in, by size and color, into different shoe boxes.

Grace was poring over a diagram that she had drawn on a big sheet of graph paper. Each part of the chicken's body had been outlined and labeled with the type of battery that was to fill it, and how they were to be arranged. For example, the eye was to be made of silver watch batteries in a spiral pattern. Now she was using white chalk to sketch the diagram over the map.

Miss Rosenweig handed out bottles of Elmer's glue. "Peiling, why don't you start on the head? Sandra and I will work on the wings and—"

Baba walked in. Peiling looked up in surprise. "I left

work early, because I thought you might need some help," he explained. "I brought these, too." He opened his briefcase and pulled out a couple of hot-glue guns. "Some of those batteries are pretty heavy. I'm not sure ordinary glue will be strong enough to hold them."

Holding a glue gun in each hand, he looked like one of the gunfighters who showed up to save the day in those movies about the Old West. Even as she fought back the urge to giggle, Peiling also felt a strange surge of pride. "Thanks, Baba," she said.

Grace, who had been looking doubtfully at the Elmer's, gave a smile that lit up her face. "Thanks, Mr. Wang!" She plugged in a glue gun and began to glue rectangular nine-volt batteries in an interlocking brick pattern to make the feet. Baba plugged the other one in and started to help Peiling with the head.

The door flew open with a bang. It was Mrs. Baldino, out of breath and wild-eyed.

"Oh, thank God!" she gasped, leaning on the door frame. "Laura said you might be here. We're doing the final run-through of the play for tomorrow night, and the school nurse just told me that Simon got sent home with pinkeye!"

She stumbled over to Peiling and took her by the shoulders. "Peiling, you'll have to play the part. Oh, thank goodness I had you learn the pauper's lines!"

Miss Rosenweig stared at Mrs. Baldino, slightly bewildered by this outburst. Then she nodded slowly and said, "Oh, I see. Peiling is the pauper's understudy. Well, then, you'd better go with Mrs. Baldino."

Suddenly, Peiling felt as lightheaded as if the classroom had been sucked of oxygen. Simon Pence with pinkeye! She, Peiling Wang, would actually star in the school play! A part of her hesitated, wanting to stay and help the others with the collage. Despite, or maybe because of, all its ups and downs, she had become attached to the project, and wanted to see it to the end.

But at the same time, the tiny flame that had burned inside of her ever since she had first read the pauper's part at that rehearsal in early December flared up into life inside her. She wanted to play the part. She looked uncertainly at Grace and Baba. They nodded reassuringly.

"Don't worry. Everything's under control here," Grace said, nudging her.

Before Peiling could respond, Mrs. Baldino tugged her by the hand out of the classroom and whisked her down the hallway to the auditorium. The whole cast was in costume. Matt and Madeline were in their places onstage waiting for her, while Laura was pacing nervously between them.

"Thank heaven!" she exclaimed, when she saw Peiling. She ran over and helped Mrs. Baldino get Peiling into the pauper's costume. "Here's my script," she said, handing Peiling a battered stack of stapled copies. "I don't need it."

Peiling waved it away, taking a deep breath. "Neither do I."

She walked onstage between Madeline and Matt. "Oh, Father," she began. "I brought home only a farthing, although I begged all day up and down Mincing Lane . . ."

The rest of the rehearsal was a blur. The pauper's lines, which she had practiced so painstakingly alone in her room all through December and January, seemed to come effortlessly to her lips when she was onstage with the others.

At the end of the last act, Mrs. Baldino almost threw herself into Peiling's arms. "Oh, Peiling. We'll need to do an emergency rehearsal tomorrow afternoon, but I do believe you're going to save my play after all."

She put a hand to her head. "Oh, dear. All this excitement has given me a splitting headache. I'm afraid I'm going to have to go home and take a couple of aspirin and put a hot water bottle on my head." She tottered out.

The rest of the cast changed out of their costumes and started to drift away as their rides arrived. Peiling took off the pauper's costume and was about to go back to Miss Rosenweig's classroom, when Laura, the only one still there, stopped her.

"How'd you know the pauper's lines so well?" she demanded accusingly.

"Mrs. Baldino asked me back in December to memorize them."

"Oh, really?" Laura said, nodding as if Peiling had admitted to a dark crime. "Well, you certainly did a good job of keeping quiet about it all this time." Laura shook her head. "Peiling Wang, you certainly are an odd duck. If it were me, *I* wouldn't have kept quiet about it. *I* would have wanted everyone to know."

She looked at Peiling curiously. "How come you're not more of a show-off? Whenever you've done something special, you never tell anyone about it, like when that essay you wrote about immigrants in Cleveland was published in the paper. People only found out about it because Grace said something. And now this . . ."

Peiling felt uncomfortable. "You should only worry about doing your best, not about impressing other people. At least, that's what my parents taught me. In fact, they say it's better if people underestimate you a little."

Laura laughed. "But what's the big deal if people think you're better than you are? I know that when I try out for something, I'm more likely to get the part if people have heard good things about me, even if I don't have a good audition."

Abruptly she changed the subject. "Are you nervous about tomorrow night? There's a big difference between saying your lines at rehearsal and the real performance, you know."

Peiling looked out at the empty auditorium. She pictured all the seats, instead of being empty, being filled with rows and rows of strangers' faces. A part of her shrank with panic, but another part of her felt giddy with excitement. She wanted to speak to those unfamiliar faces. She wanted to make them smile with delight and tremble with fear, even if she didn't know their names. "I think I'll be all right," she said.

Laura nodded wisely. "Yeah, well, I guess the adrenaline will carry you through, anyhow. I remember the first time I starred in a play. I was so nervous that I couldn't sleep for two nights. I was a total wreck. But once I got onstage, I was wide awake, and didn't miss a line."

She paused and smiled wryly. "I love being onstage. You know why I like it so much? Because if I know my lines, then I know that everything will go smoothly. Not like in real life, when it seems like I'm always saying the wrong thing. Like that day after Christmas vacation when I made you so mad. Do you remember?"

Of course Peiling remembered. She nodded.

"I didn't really mean to hurt your feelings," Laura said. "I was just being jealous, I guess."

Peiling figured that this was the closest thing to an apology she could expect from Laura. "That's okay," she said awkwardly.

"Well, anyway, I'd better go now. Make sure you get a good night's sleep. It also helps if you gargle with salt water to keep your vocal chords supple," she said, snapping back to know-it-all mode. Laura ran out the door, leaving Peiling to make her way slowly back to the classroom.

16

Laura was right. Adrenaline carried Peiling through. From the moment the curtain rose on the first act, a manic, concentrated energy possessed her. Her body felt limber and graceful, and her lines came effortlessly and unthinkingly to her lips. She felt as if nothing existed beyond the four corners of the stage—not the audience, not Simon Pence, not Mrs. Baldino hyperventilating in the wings. She felt neither nervous nor tired. All she was aware of was the blinding glare of the stage lights and the voices of the other actors echoing confusedly around her.

It was only when the curtain rose on the final act that time seemed to slow from its breakneck rush. Her eyes accustomed themselves to the stage lights, her heart stopped racing, and she was finally able to notice what was going on around her.

The pauper was about to be declared King of England. The gold-sequined crown was being lowered onto Peiling's head. With a resounding bang, the double doors of Westminster Abbey flew open. Laura, mud-stained and out of breath, burst in. "Halt!" she cried. "I forbid you to set the Crown of England upon that head. I am king!"

The palace guards rushed forward to eject Laura. Peiling sprang up from the throne. "Loose him and forbear!" she shouted, her voice ringing through the silent auditorium. Then she rushed forward and threw herself at Laura's feet. "Now, O my King, take these regal garments back, and give poor Tom, thy servant, his shreds and remnants again!" she cried.

Now, for the first time, although she had recited the words dozens of times before, she understood why Tom Canty would speak them. Whenever he had tried to explain who he really was, no one believed him. They even thought he was crazy. For the first time in his life, he had enough to eat and a warm place to sleep. But instead of being grateful, he missed his mother and sisters, and dreamed of being reunited with them in his old, wretched hovel.

Tears welled up in Peiling's eyes, and it was through their confused blur that she watched the remainder of the scene: the story of the exchanged garments told, the proofs of Edward's identity given. At last, Laura, the true king, stepped forward to claim the crown, amid joyous cries of "Long live the king!" from the crowd onstage.

The curtain fell. Peiling, exhausted, slumped into the throne.

"Let's go!" Laura grabbed her hand and pulled her to her feet.

"What is it?"

"Curtain call. We have to make our bows."

The curtain rose again. Laura dragged Peiling to the front of the stage. The rest of the cast lined up on either side of them. Mrs. Baldino tottered out, blushing and nodding at the thunderous applause. She burst into tears when the cast presented her with a huge bouquet of red roses, and now she was laughing and blowing her nose at the same time.

Peiling squinted out over the footlights to scan the rows of the applauding audience. It took her a minute to find what she was looking for. In row three was a line of heads with hair as black and straight as her own. It was Mama and Baba and the aunties and uncles on their feet, clapping and waving. Grace was standing on her seat beside them, stamping her feet and sticking her pinkies in her mouth to whistle.

Peiling turned to look at Laura. Their mingled sweat made their hands slippery, but still their fingers were interlocked. Laura's crown was almost sliding off the black wig that she had agreed to wear so she would look more like Peiling. She looked pretty good as a brunette, actually. They smiled at each other.

Mrs. Baldino had finally managed to compose herself. Now, as the applause died down, she stepped forward to the front of the stage to make an announcement. "Parents, friends, students, thank you for coming! Now, will everyone please join us for tea and cookies in the Main Hall, where the Winter Projects will be on display."

Breathlessly, Peiling rushed backstage with Laura to take off her costume. Then they hurried together to the Main Hall.

The first thing Peiling noticed was a crowd of people clustered around something on the wall. Squeezing through, Peiling saw what they were looking at. Filling a five-foot–square expanse of the wall was the collage, triumphantly labeled, "How the World Celebrates, Miss Rosenweig, Fifth Grade." The brilliant tapestry of the continents was brought out by the black velvet of the ocean. In the foreground, the giant rooster gleamed boldly. The edge of its comb was picked out in metallic red. Its wings were made of copper cylinders rimmed with black. Its tail was a cascading fan of silver double-A's.

"Absolutely gorgeous," someone in the crowd said.

"How creative," another added. "Have you ever seen anything so original?"

Next to the collage was Mr. Guy's Winter Project, but no one seemed interested in that, except for a pimply teenage boy. Peiling edged closer so she could see it better. On a square of linoleum, lit by the flickering of red and green strobe lights, was an empty armchair. A pair of shabby blue slippers rested on the floor before it. To the side was an end table with a half-drunk mug of coffee. Six feet in front of the chair was a black-and-white TV with old-fashioned rabbit-ear antennae.

One by one the members of Mr. Guy's class flashed on-screen. "Christmas is . . . ," Britney intoned, "getting together with friends and family." The music was a hip-hop version of "We Three Kings." In the background, Peiling could recognize Mr. Guy's voice interjecting an occasional "Yo!" or "Word up!"

The teenage boy wasn't even listening. He was staring at the black-and-white TV. "What is this? Some kind of antique or something?" he muttered to himself.

"Peiling! Laura!" someone called through the crowd. Peiling turned. It was Mrs. Hamilton. She held two bouquets of flowers, one for each of them. "Peiling, you were wonderful!" she said, giving Peiling a big hug. Then she hugged Laura.

A tall, thin man with large teeth came up to them. "Hello, Peiling, I'm Laura's dad," he said. "I've heard so much about you."

"Nice to meet you, Mr. Hamilton," Peiling said.

"That's Dr. Hamilton," Laura corrected. "He's an orthodontist."

Now Mama and Baba and the aunties and uncles were there. They didn't hug her, but Mama smoothed the hair on her brow. "You did a wonderful job, Peiling. You were very expressive," she said.

Baba bent down and said in Chinese. "I'm proud of you. You know, my aunt is the mayor of Gaoxiong city. When you were up there, speaking so loudly and clearly, you reminded me of her."

Mr. Hamilton came over with his hand extended. "You must be Peiling's parents!" he said smiling. "I'm Laura's dad."

He shook Baba's hand. "You know, we love Chinese food, and we hear that your wife is some cook. What do you think of Sun Luck Gardens?"

"Sun Luck Gardens?" Peiling felt herself tense up. She saw Baba's lips tighten, and his nostrils flare. Then Baba forced a crooked smile. "Their food is . . . not bad, not bad at all." He paused. Peiling saw him unclenching his fist. "But why don't you give Li Hua a try? I think their food is, shall we say, more authentic."

Mr. Hamilton was pulling a ballpoint pen and scrap of paper out of his pocket so Baba could give him directions.

Mama and Mrs. Hamilton were standing next to each other. Mama turned to Mrs. Hamilton and said with her slight accent, "Laura was really good. Your daughter's very talented."

"Thank you," Mrs. Hamilton said. "And Peiling did an amazing job, especially considering she didn't have time to rehearse, and only found out she was going on yesterday!"

She leaned closer to Mama and added in an undervoice, "But mostly, I'm so happy the two girls have become friends. You know, Laura doesn't make new friends easily. And Peiling's such a good example for her."

"Peiling?" Mama said in surprise.

"Yes," Mrs. Hamilton nodded vigorously. "Peiling doesn't have to be the center of attention, but she knows who she is and doesn't let herself get pushed around."

"Really," said Mama. She paused, and said with difficulty, "We've worried a lot about Peiling since we've come to the States."

"You shouldn't," said Mrs. Hamilton, patting Mama's hand. "You've done a great job with her."

Suddenly Peiling caught sight of Uncle Samson coming over, holding a large bouquet of yellow tulips.

"Uncle Samson! I didn't know you were here!" she said, throwing herself into his arms.

She missed him so much. He and Mama had still not made up their quarrel. She hadn't seen him since Chinese New Year.

"Did you think I'd miss your school play?" he said. "Peiling, you were terrific!"

"Aren't you going to come by the house anymore?" she whispered, hugging him tightly.

"Of course," he smiled at her reassuringly.

Miss Rosenweig popped out from behind him. "Super job, Peiling!"

Shyly holding open her arms as her teacher leaned down to give her a kiss, Peiling noticed over Miss Rosenweig's shoulder that Uncle Samson, instead of moving away, just stood there, looking nonchalant. Her eye fell on the brown velvet coat draped over his arm and the green bike helmet dangling from his wrist. An unexpected thought occurred to her, spiraling dizzily up inside her like a bubble of joy.

Her eyes moved from Uncle Samson to Miss Rosenweig. She was smiling and radiant. A glittery scarf of metallic gold lace framed her flushed face, and her long brown hair, which she usually wore in a lopsided ponytail, curled over her shoulders.

"Miss Rosenweig!" Laura squealed, catching sight of their teacher and throwing herself into Miss Rosenweig's arms.

Under cover of Laura's excited chatter, Peiling sidled up to Uncle Samson.

"You didn't ask her out?"

He nodded, a smile crinkling the corners of his eyes.

"And she said yes?" Peiling said incredulously.

Uncle Samson said, "Shut up, Peiling," but he didn't sound angry.

"I can't believe it!"

"Why not?" He was watching Miss Rosenweig nod and smile as Laura babbled on so enthusiastically that her wig almost fell off. "She's a rabbit, and I'm a boar. Boars and rabbits get along. At least, that's what that book said."

"What book?"

"You know. The one your mother got her about the Chinese zodiac." Uncle Samson grinned.

"I'll see you in school on Monday, Laura," Miss Rosenweig said firmly. She had finally managed to detach herself from Laura, and had come back to Peiling and Uncle Samson.

"Ready to go, Deanna?" Uncle Samson said.

"Okay."

While Uncle Samson helped Miss Rosenweig with her coat, she smiled confidentially at Peiling. "I'll see you before Monday," she said. "We're coming to your house for dinner this Saturday."

She crouched down a little so her face was at Peiling's level. "Tell your mother this time I'm bringing the chicken-fried steak," she said.

Her face was expressionless, even blank, but her right eyelid on the side facing Uncle Samson deliberately dropped and opened again in a perfect wink.

17

Peiling was too excited to sleep. Long after they had come home from the play, long after she had brushed her teeth and turned out the light, she lay in bed awake. She stared up at the ceiling, watching the shadows of the trees slide over the walls and ceiling every time a car came up the street. Finally, she gave up trying to go to sleep. She got up and turned on the lamp. She stuck her head out into the hallway. The whole house was dark and silent. She heard the gentle snores of Mama and Baba from their room down the hall.

She sat down at the desk in her room. She opened the drawer and pulled out the program from the play. It was lettered in old-fashioned calligraphy and printed on stiff, yellowish paper that was supposed to look like parchment. At the bottom of "Cast of Characters," the only mention of her was "Pauper's Understudy: Peiling Wang." She would keep it forever to remind her of this night.

As she was putting the program back in the drawer, her fingers brushed against the rough cover of the book Miss Rosenweig had given her for Christmas. She took it out of the drawer. With her index finger she gently traced the shape of the fern fronds and the rose petals. She opened it to the first page. For a long time, she looked at its smooth blankness. Suddenly, she had an idea.

She padded downstairs in her bare feet. The shades hadn't been drawn, and the family room looked mysterious and shadowy in the light from the street. She fumbled her way to the bookshelf. Half by feel she found the magazine she had given Mama at Christmas. She hugged it to her chest and ran upstairs to her room.

Kneeling beside her bed, she flipped through the glossy pages, looking for the recipe for chicken-fried steak. She found it, superimposed over a full-page close-up of the fried cutlets, garnished with cherry tomatoes and sprigs of parsley. Underneath the recipe, Mama had written in her firm, tight script, "Add pinch of five-spice powder to the coating."

Peiling sat down at her desk. She smoothed the magazine page in front of her. She dug around in the drawer for a felt-tip pen. On the very first page of the book from Miss Rosenweig, she wrote in capital letters an inch high:

WANG FAMILY CHRISTMAS RECIPES

On the next page, she copied the recipe from the magazine, incorporating Mama's changes:

2 pounds top round steak
1 egg
¾ cup milk

2 cups flour
1 teaspoon salt
1 teaspoon black pepper
pinch of five-spice powder
2 cups vegetable oil

Pound steaks on both sides with meat pounder until even thickness. Season with salt and pepper. Whisk together egg and milk in a shallow dish. In another shallow dish, whisk together flour, salt, pepper, and five-spice powder. Dip steak in egg mixture, and then dredge in flour mixture. Heat oil in a deep skillet until hot but not smoking. Fry steak in batches, turning over once, until golden brown.

Smiling, Peiling read it over. Then she shut the book and slid it under her mattress for next year.